CLIPPED

A KINGS MC ROMANCE

WINGS

BETTY
SHREFFLER

CLIPPED WINGS

Published by Betty Shreffler

Editor: Sandy Ebel—Personal Touch Editing

www.facebook.com/PersonalTouchEditing/

❀ Created with Vellum

CHAPTER ONE

ERIKA

MY FINGERS SPLAY around the copper knob of my door, slowly opening it to an array of stimulations. Music thumps, vibrating my chest and ears. Stepping out, I'm accosted by a thick, grey cloud of smoke lingering just below the ceiling. The aroma of marijuana and sex are scents I'm used to in my home. My mother, Dori and my sister, Amberlee act like sisters rather than mother and daughter, and the front door of our shitty ranch home is a revolving movement of men in and men out.

Tonight is no different from most weekends, except this time my sister's new boyfriend is a member of a biker gang, the Devil's Serpents. They're as scary as the name sounds. Most of the members lounging in my living room frighten me, except one—Dominic. When his eyes follow me across the room, my skin burns with an unfamiliar heat. Between my legs, I ache with a want so fierce, it startles me.

Crossing the living room filled with blunts and beer cans, I make my way to our small, worn out, tacky yellow kitchen. Dominic's bold, jade eyes glisten like a hungry lion, gaze dead set on its prey. Maybe I should be afraid, he looks like he's six-foot-something, muscles on every inch of his body, tats covering every part of his skin I see, except his face and neck. He could easily overpower me, force me down, and rape me, and there's nothing I could do about it, but the fucked-up part, I get turned on thinking about him dominating me.

Sucking my lip between my teeth, I tear my gaze off his intriguing eyes, chiseled jaw, and dark, short brown hair. The blast of the cool refrigerator melts my fiery libido, and I reach in for a bottle of water. Yeah, I'm the lame sister. The one who doesn't party, smoke pot, or get plastered on alcohol and can't remember who I fucked the night before. I'm still a virgin, and it's something my sister gets a kick out of telling all her new friends. She might as well pin a target to my back with the kind of people she hangs around with. I have no interest in apologizing for my virginity. Just because she lost her virginity at fifteen and never stopped spreading her legs to every guy who looked her way doesn't mean I have to.

Amberlee and I are polar opposites. I read books, she uses the pages to make her own cigarettes. I like to eat healthy, she lives on pop and chips and doesn't gain a damn pound. She likes loud rock-and-roll music at all times of the day and night, I like to have peace and quiet to think and sleep. She constantly needs attention from friends and boyfriends, I can count my close friends on one hand and boyfriends even less. Every boyfriend I've ever brought home ends up being Amberlee's fuck toy for the night. Great sister, right?

There was a time when we were close, but after our dad went to jail, she and mom spiraled out of control. My mom, Dori is even worse. She's not even home half the time. She works nights at a twenty-four-hour diner, and when she is home, she's not really "home." Her drugs are more important than paying rent sometimes. Thankfully, Amberlee keeps her head on straight enough to pay any bills my mother "forgets" to pay. She dropped out of college her second year and has been working at beauty salons or in retail ever since. She's been fired a couple times, but I'm thankful this last place seems to be working for her.

I only have three months until I start community college, and it can't come fast enough. If my mother and sister have taught me anything, it's I don't want to be like them. I want to move out of this shithole and make a life for myself, in a town far, far away where no one knows me or the family I come from.

Being the daughter of a drug dealer and murderer in a small town puts a serious damper on your social life. Most people view our family as the trash of Cinderville, Ohio. People spread rumor after rumor, and before long, the rumors become truth, and no one cares to know otherwise. That's probably why I've never had a long-lasting boyfriend. Most have either slept with my sister, or if they haven't, they're probably a good guy, but I'm not *good enough* for them. They know my family, take one look at me and assume I'm the same.

Maybe I am like my family, or maybe I haven't been given the chance to spread my wings. Either way, they can kiss my ass. I don't need judgmental pricks in my life. It's crazy enough as it is. I've had to grow up a hell of a lot faster than they have and have seen things that would make them squirm in their khakis.

Closing the refrigerator door, I untwist the bottle cap and pour the refreshing cold liquid down my throat. My grip tightens on the bottle when a hand snakes over my hip and languidly strokes the top of my jean shorts.

"Erika, right?"

A pelvis is thrust into my ass, and I'm shoved into the refrigerator, my patience teetering on a thin layer. Sadly, this isn't the first time I've had one of Dori's or Amberlee's friends make a move on me. With a quick hip thrust, I knock him off my ass. Turning, I glare at the dirty, old fuck, shoving his hand away.

"Not interested. Hands *off*."

He's not getting the hint. Pinning me against the refrigerator, his dark brown gaze slithers over the V of my shirt and chest. The stench of stale cigarette and beer is heavy with this one. An unwanted, abrasive hand squeezes my ass, yanking me closer to his crotch.

"I like a woman with sass. Makes it more fun in the bedroom."

My nails dig into his arm, his grip tightens, but I slam my palm down on his forearm and his grip falters. With one quick and angry slap, his hand goes to his cheek and my fingers are left with a burning sting.

"I'm *not* interested. *Back off.*"

Storming off, my bottle goes flying through the air and hits the counter, then the floor as two hands latch onto my arms, yanking me back into the kitchen. Water pools in a puddle as I'm shoved into the counter, the air escaping me.

I groan, and he laughs. "Thought you could walk away from me, didn't you, bitch?"

The loud music thunders in my ears, matching the hard beat in my chest. When his hand reaches for my jean shorts and fists them, I'm whipped around, facing his seething scowl and determined stare.

"Now get on your knees and show me how sorry you are."

Fear seizes me as I look over his shoulder. No one gives a shit what's going on in the kitchen. Amberlee is nowhere to be seen, probably in her room fucking her boyfriend, Ditch. Dori's at work tonight, and even if she was here, she'd be strung out and useless. I'm alone, as usual, to handle this problem. A problem I shouldn't have to be dealing with in my own home.

Reaching behind me, I cover my moving arm with my body as I search for anything to hit or stab this fucker with. My hand touches metal, I don't know what it is, but I grip it tight and swing.

My arm stops mid-air, my wrist ringing in pain from the hand gripping it.

"She's off limits, Tex. That was the deal."

Dominic's grip eases on my wrist, and I lower the can opener.

Tex and Dominic stare each other down. Dominic towers several inches over Tex's bulbous frame. His gaze is ruthless, his eyes display a challenge he seems ready to fulfill.

Tex drops his shoulders. "The bitch hit me. I was gonna teach the slut a lesson."

"I'll take care of it," Dominic declares. The tone of his voice sends a chill over my skin. Not the way Tex's touch did either. It's arousing and frightening all at once.

"You fucking better," Tex demands.

Tex takes one last look at me and sneers. "You're gonna wish you sucked my cock, you little whore."

My eyes narrow at his back as he walks away. Raising my arm, I'm ready to release the can opener at the back of his head. Dominic grips my wrist again, his massive frame filling my vision.

"Drop it, now," he orders.

My fingers loosen instantly, and the can opener falls into his waiting palm.

"That's a good girl."

Reaching around me, his gaze remains steady on my eyes as he sets the can opener somewhere behind me.

"You need to be smart around these bastards. They'll hurt you and won't give a fuck how much you cry."

The heat of his gaze burns over my skin. The anger and hatred I feel are melting away the longer he lingers over me.

"Now I know. Next time, I'll start sucking a stranger's cock, no questions asked."

Dominic's laugh is a melodic sound of danger mixed with sexy.

"I'm not saying you need to whore yourself out. I'm saying be smart, use your head, not your knuckles."

"Why do you care? Why did you stop him?" I ask, curious.

"Not sure yet. Maybe you'll give me a reason to."

So, I've exchanged one asshole for another.

"I don't think so. I don't sleep with Dori or Amberlee's friends."

Dominic's fingers graze my chin, then pull my face upward, holding my gaze hostage to his.

"So I've heard. Why don't you?"

Hand gripping the counter, his arm blocks my movement right, and his body, my left. I'm pinned between him and the counter, and I'm burning up with an outrageous desire to feel his lips on mine.

"I have no interest in being used. I respect myself."

Dominic's tongue swipes over his lips, his breath warm, brushing across my mouth.

"That's good. Real good," his words are a smooth whisper across my lips.

I've been kissed before, but I've never felt a desire quite like this. Dominic's masculinity is incredibly arousing. I should feel terrified of him, but oddly, I don't. More than anything, I feel compelled to submit to know what it feels like to be kissed by a man this handsome, this dangerous, this seductive.

The thunderous music and chaos bustle around us as his tongue invades my mouth. My stiff body goes slack in the arm folding around my back. I'm dragged to his chest, my hands finding the ridges of his shoulders and biceps. My ass touches the counter as he pushes forward. His towering frame engulfs me, holding me to him as his tongue makes skilled movements over mine.

My mind goes blank, our surroundings become a blur as his masculinity invades my senses. His mouth is methodical, moving my lips to his tempo, and I'm pliant in this dance. With a fist in my hair, Dominic pulls my head back, his kiss pushing me toward an antagonizing level of unfamiliar need.

My jean shorts are gripped in his other hand, a bulge in his jeans pressing into me. A startling growl slips between his lips.

Behind him, I'm saved from my total loss of control by the voice of one of his biker friends.

"Dom, you'll have to fuck that chick later. I need you for a run."

Unhurriedly, Dominic withdraws from our kiss. My swollen lips tingle the moment we part. His grip doesn't loosen as he leans his head next to my ear.

"See you around."

CHAPTER TWO

ERIKA

MY ROOM IS where I usually stay for Amberlee's parties, but tonight it's extra rowdy. On the other side of my door, I hear scuffling, then glass shatters against the wall. Frowning, I move to the door and look out. Blood spatter is smeared across the wall and standing over a bloody, knocked out Serpent is Dominic. His gaze is deadly and his knuckles crimson red. He takes one careless glance at me and walks off, his chest rising and falling with his breaths.

Amberlee is sitting on Ditch's lap in the living room, admiring the scene.

"He tore his ass up," she laughs.

Ditch's pierced brow raises with his smirk before taking a drink of his beer.

Stepping out of my room, I lean down to check if the guy is conscious.

"Leave him," Dominic barks.

I jolt at the commanding sound of his voice just before he disappears into our bathroom.

Stepping over the guy, I follow Dominic. Amberlee's gaze watches me, then is stolen away by Ditch pulling her attention to him.

"Don't worry about it," is all I hear him say.

Cautiously cracking the door open, I see Dominic's reflection in the mirror. Those bold jade eyes hold me steady. Heat rises up my neck. It's been a week since I've seen Dominic, and seeing him now in my bathroom, his muscles damp and tight from the fight has my body buzzing with sensitivity.

"Don't be worried about a piece of shit like that."

With a slight movement of his head, the light catches the lethal look in his eyes I saw moments ago. Again, I should be afraid, and yet, I'm still drawn like a moth to a flame. Stepping into the bathroom, I close the door behind us.

"What happened?"

Dominic laughs. It's dangerously controlled. "It's club business."

His magnetizing gaze pulls away. Reaching for a towel, he turns to face me.

"How old are you?"

"Twenty," I blurt out. It's stupid, I know, but I don't want him to know my real age. I don't want him to look at me differently than he is now.

His eyes survey me, roaming over my face and body before stopping at the tattoo peeking out of my shorts.

Tossing the towel behind him, he folds his arms. "What's the tattoo? Show me, all of it."

"Amberlee's ex-boyfriend gave us both tattoos." Unbuttoning my shorts, I unzip them and fold them down, revealing all the ink. "It's a sparrow."

Dominic's boots thud across the floor as he takes the few steps, closing the distance between us. With his thumb, he traces the ink. Goosebumps raise over my skin with each stroke of his finger. Putting his free hand on my neck, he grips and pulls me close, my head forced to look up at him.

"If anyone else asks to see that tattoo, tell 'em to fuck off, don't unbutton your shorts like you just did for me."

Lips slamming down on mine, his tongue whips into my mouth, pulling my lust to the surface. My body hums with an uncontrollable need. Gripping my hips, he raises me with ease. My legs wrap around his waist, then loosen as he sets me on the sink.

"You're too pretty for your own damn good."

"You think I'm pretty?"

"I wouldn't be wanting to stick my cock in you if I didn't think so."

Taking my hand in his, Dominic places it over the bulge in his jeans.

"Feel that? I'm getting hard thinking about it."

Surprised by the size of him, I withdraw my hand, my eyes wide.

The corner of his mouth lifts. "Never felt a cock that big?"

Shaking my head, Dominic laughs. "You might be bold, but beneath that tough exterior, you're innocent and naive."

"I'm not naive," I snap back.

Arms braced on each side of me, Dominic stares into my eyes. The intensity excites me as much as it rattles me.

"You put yourself in a room alone with me, you're naive."

"What if I want to be alone with you?"

"What do you think is gonna happen if we stay in here?"

"I don't know."

Dominic's finger grazes over my tattoo before he grips my shorts.

"Yes, you do. You keep walking around looking at me with those fuck me eyes, your body begs for more each time I kiss you, and you've got your shorts unbuttoned, teasing me. So, what's it going to be?"

Brushing my hair off my shoulder, he grips my neck as he comes torturously close to my lips.

"You want my cock filling your tight hole? Want me to cum all over your ass?"

His bold words arouse me even more. My body is

begging to be touched, to have this ache sated, yet there are annoying thoughts entering my mind. *How bad will it hurt? Or will it? Will he know I'm a virgin? Will he be able to tell?*

"Yes," the word slips from my mouth before I realize what I've said.

A wicked smirk crosses his face. My hands grasp his shoulders as he lifts me from the sink. His mouth smothers my excited whimper as he pulls my shorts off my hips. My underwear quickly follows, leaving me bare in only my shirt and bra.

I have no time to think much of my nudity as my arms instinctively raise. Dominic's fingers graze along my skin as he lifts my shirt over my chest. Tossing my shirt, he stares at my cleavage and pink bra.

"Jesus, these tits."

His eyes catch the clasp in the front and he goes for it, releasing my breasts, letting the bra flutter to the floor.

Cupping my left breast in his hand, he lifts it, filling his mouth with my nipple. My head falls back and my breathing increases in raspy, needy whimpers.

Reaching down, he slides his fingers between my legs and I cry out in pleasure.

"Fuck, you're soaking wet for me. You want my cock more than I thought."

"I do," I plead, writhing over his fingers.

He adds another digit and my mouth forms an 'O' as I moan.

"Like my fingers fucking you?"

"Yes."

"Say how much you like it," he demands.

Gripping the sink, I squeeze as he adds a third digit, stretching me.

"You feel so good. I want more."

"I'm gonna give you more. So much more."

The warm touch of his hand leaves my breast, and I hear the zipper of his jeans come undone.

Glancing down, I watch him stroke his erection, and the sight of it turns me on. Dominic's lascivious gaze matches mine as he continues fisting and working his erection.

"Want to put your mouth on it?"

Nibbling my lip, I nod, "I do."

"That a girl."

I might be a virgin, but it's not my first time being intimate. I've done everything but give up the v-card. Why I want to give it to Dominic, I don't know. There's something about him that makes me want to pleasure him and take every bit of pleasure he's willing to give.

Taking him in my hand, I admire how thick and long he is. His cock is perfect. A single vein stretching across the top, thickening as I place my mouth on his head.

Curling his fingers around my hair, he tightens his grip as I move him in and out, taking him to the back of my throat, sucking hard, then repeating it with an eager moan.

"Like that, don't you?"

Looking up at his satisfied expression, I suck harder. Dominic pulls back with a hiss.

"Fuuuck, suck any harder and I'm gonna cum in your mouth and miss the feeling of your tight pussy."

Tugging at his black tank, he pulls it over his head, revealing all the intricate ink. Black designs go every which way. My eyes can't settle on one design, they roam over his body, admiring every skull, flower, star, cross, and tribal design.

"You like what you see?"

"Yes."

Beneath his glossy green eyes, the curl of his lip tells me he's pleased to hear that. Looking me up and down, I suddenly feel self-conscious being naked. Crossing my arms over my chest, I try to cover myself somewhat as his gaze blazes a heated trail across my skin.

Dominic takes my arms in his hands, stopping me from covering myself.

"Look at me."

Lifting me, he sets me on the sink. The cold porcelain is a stark contrast to his warm hands. Keeping my gaze locked on his, he takes his erection in his hand, guiding it between my spread legs. I flinch at the unfamiliar sensation, then instantly relax as he moves his head against my wet opening.

The motion sets my body on fire, my need rises, yearning for more. His dominating mouth takes control, his tongue sliding between my lips as his cock pushes forward, filling me.

Slowly at first, he slides out a little, then back in. I feel myself stretching around him, a warm discomfort but tolerable. My body is confused on what to focus on, his incredible kiss, or the new sensation between my legs. His pace picks up, and my ass rocks over the sink. Keeping hold of my ass, he holds me steady as he pumps into me.

"This pussy... so fucking tight."

Claiming my mouth, he puts a hand under my leg, raising it in the air, positioning himself deeper in. Clinging to him, I hold my breath as his thrusts get harder. The slick sound of our bodies slapping together echoes through the small bathroom, and I bite my lip as his cock pounds against my cervix.

"Goddamn, you feel so fucking good. I want to come in your ass."

The statement shocks me, and he seems to notice.

His thrusts slow. "Never had anal, have you?"

Shaking my head, he gives a humored chuckle. "That's ok. Don't worry about it."

Dropping my leg, he pulls out and the warmth of him abruptly leaves me, leaving behind a cold and hollow feeling.

"Turn around."

Across my back, his strong hand warms my skin, then with ease he pushes me forward. Bracing my hands on the sink, I glance over my shoulder and see the satisfied look on his face as he pumps his erection in his fist. Hot cum shoots across my ass and back. With the last of it, he squeezes my ass.

"Fuck, that was good."

Dominic reaches over me, grabbing the towel from the sink and wipes his hand on it. He goes silent, wiping the towel between my legs, across my back, helping to clean me off.

"Are you on your period?" he asks, his tone suddenly uneasy.

"No."

Grip tight on my arm, he turns me to face him. "There's blood on me and the towel. Were you a virgin before this?"

It's hard to hold his gaze, he seems irritated.

"Jesus fucking Christ, you were, weren't you?"

"What does it matter?"

My arms cover my chest as I squat down and scoop up my clothes.

"If I'd known," Dominic pushes me back with his dominating presence, "I wouldn't have fucked you in this bathroom."

A hysterical knock pounds at the door. "Dominic, why are you still in there with Erika?"

It's Amberlee.

Dominic rakes a hand through his hair and lets out a frustrated growl through his teeth. Tucking himself back into his jeans, he zips them, then cracks the door. Amberlee tries to push through, and he easily contains her.

"What the fuck are you doing? She's barely eighteen," Amberlee shouts.

Looking past her, he speaks to someone behind her. "Ditch, get your woman under control. Stay the fuck out of my business, Alee."

"Alee, leave them alone. C'mon."

"Asshole," she barks, just before he slams the door in her face.

Dominic turns to me. His jaw is twitching beneath darkened eyes.

"You said you were twenty. *Twenty*," he snaps.

I jump at the raised tone of his voice.

"When did you turn eighteen?"

"Four months ago."

"Fuck, no wonder Alee's pissed."

Embarrassed, I clutch the towel and my clothes to my naked body. With him standing between me and the door, I can't escape this awkward situation. Tears pool in my eyes as the expression on Dominic's face turns to disgust.

"You lied to me. I *don't* tolerate being lied to."

"I'm sorry."

"Get in the shower."

"Why," I ask, startled.

"Because I said to. Do you want to piss me off any more than you already have?"

I drop my clothes and reach for the knob of the shower, turning it to a heated temperature. Dominic locks the bathroom door, then strips down, removing all his clothes.

"Get in," he orders.

Uncomfortable with his brooding mood and demanding orders, I reluctantly step into the shower. Dominic's muscles are tense as he steps in behind me. His jaw still tight.

"You have a woman's body, but you're still immature."

His comment stings.

"You should've told me you were only eighteen and a virgin."

I feel Dominic's scolding gaze more than the hot water. Pushing me under the water, he reaches for the soap bottle behind me. Stepping toward him, I move my head out of the water as he's squeezing soap into his hand.

"Would it have made a difference?"

Dominic scoffs. "Maybe."

"So, you wouldn't have had sex with me if you knew I was eighteen and a virgin?"

"It doesn't matter what I would've done now. I've already been inside your pussy."

"I liked having you inside me."

Dominic surprises me by running his hands over my body, lathering me with soap. Reaching between my legs, I inhale a shocked breath, and his wicked smirk widens as he soaps me up.

"Don't be modest now. As for sex, it gets better. I

might've been more gentle had I known." Dominic hands me the bottle of soap and nods downward. "Wash me."

Gathering a small amount in my hand, I set the bottle aside. Placing both hands around his shaft, I soap his entire package. Staring down at me, he watches my reaction as I lather him. He appears thoroughly entertained by my fascination with his size.

"You want it again, don't you?"

My pussy is sore, but he's right. I'm getting turned on feeling him grow in my hand.

"I do."

Dominic stops my hand. "You're a temptress and don't even know it."

Stepping toward the water, he moves us both under its spray. Completely clean and feeling slightly aroused, the ache between my legs isn't as bad. I feel grateful to him for that.

"What's wrong with wanting to be with you again?"

"I haven't decided how I feel about you. You lied to me once. Means you'll do it again."

"I won't."

Dominic hums in response like my words mean nothing to him. It upsets me. Pushing the shower curtain back, I reach for a new towel off the shelf and silently step out, drying myself quickly. Wrapping the towel around me, I redress beneath it. Dominic lets out a humored laugh, pissing me off more.

"I've already seen everything."

"I don't care. You're being an ass, so now you get to see nothing."

Dominic smirks, seemingly amused by my anger. He watches me dress as he puts his clothes back on. I give him one fleeting glance before I walk out the bathroom door.

CHAPTER THREE

ERIKA

IRRITATED, I grab a beer out of the fridge and pop the top. With several gulps, I down half the bottle. Amberlee spots me and storms into the kitchen. Her golden hazel eyes, matching my own, narrow to slits. Pinching my arm between her fingers, she painfully shoves me into the shadows.

"What the fuck were you thinking giving your virginity to Dominic Xavier?"

"Keep your voice down."

"Answer me," she demands.

"I can have sex with whoever I want. I don't need your permission."

"He's the Vice President of the Serpents, Erika. He's extremely dangerous."

"Then why the hell did you invite them into our home? You weren't around when a dirty, fat, son of a bitch tried to force me to suck his cock, but Dominic was."

"So you spread your legs for him as a thank you? Is that what that was? Payment for his help? Did he make you have sex with him?"

"No, stop it. I wanted to be with him. And it was only a one-time thing. So stop acting crazy over it."

Flicking her short, auburn red hair off her shoulder, she scowls at me. "That was a stupid fucking mistake getting involved with him. I can't protect you now. You're on your own."

"Protect me? Are you kidding me? You wouldn't have to *protect* me if you didn't bring these assholes into our home in the first place."

With a flare of her nostrils, her eyes narrow. "You're a naïve, spoiled twat. The world isn't a kind place. You have to survive. I do what it takes to keep a roof over our head and food in the refrigerator."

Guilt hits me in the gut, and I bow my head. "I know you do. I appreciate that you've stepped in for Dori."

Amberlee sets her beer on the counter and leans against it next to me. "I'm sorry for being a bitch. I wish I didn't have to invite them in, but Christian Marks, the President of the Serpents is paying our bills, so our house is now his house to some extent."

"What do they get in return?"

"Don't worry about that." Amberlee runs her fingers over my hair like she did when we were kids and I was scared about our parents fighting in the other room. "That's my responsibility. Just do me a favor and don't piss off Dominic. He's got a thing about loyalty and lying."

"Shit, Alee, it's too late. He's already pissed at me."

"What? Why?"

"I told him I was twenty. Didn't tell him I was a virgin."

Amberlee chuckles, "Did he enjoy the sex?"

"Yeah."

"Then you might get lucky."

Amberlee scans the party goers. I do the same, my gaze stopping on Dominic sitting in one of the living room chairs, drinking a beer. Just the sight of him sends an arousing sensation over my body. Amberlee pushes me into the light and Dominic's attention is drawn to me. Brushing his hand over his face, he contemplates something, the wheels clearly turning.

"He wants you." Amberlee slaps my ass as she leaves the kitchen.

THE MUSIC HAS DIED DOWN to a tolerable thump outside my bedroom door, but it's not the music keeping me awake. Now that I'm alone in the confines of my room, I can't stop thinking about sex with Dominic earlier. Replaying the intimacy has me soaking wet. It's going to be difficult hiding what he does to my body every time I see him, but I'll have to try. If he's made up his mind about me, it's best I avoid him. An ache creeps into my chest at the thought of never being touched by him again. I groan against my pillow. Am I that hooked already? It's just the v-card, who gives a fuck.

Tossing to my side, I slide my hand between my legs. I'm going to need to do something about this agonizing need for release. The sound of the hinges on my door creak, and I bolt up out of bed, flicking my lamp on. Dominic closes the door behind him. Casually stepping to my bed as if he's been here before, he sits on the edge, beer dangling in his clasped hands.

"Why did you lie to me?"

His face is forward, only giving me a glimpse of his hardened expression.

Twisting a loose thread around my finger, I attempt to ease my nerves.

"I didn't want you to look at me differently than you were, and my virginity is my business. It's not something I have to tell anyone."

Dominic bows his head in thought, making a snap with his tongue, indicating he's amused or irritated. I can't tell.

"When everything is stripped from a man, all he has is his word. I don't expect you to understand with barely being an adult."

His tone is cold, reproving. I won't stand for his insults.

"Why did you come in here if you're so disgusted with my behavior?"

"Disappointed. I expect more from you."

"Fuck, you're starting to sound like a father bitching at his daughter. I have no interest in listening to you lecture me. If you don't like me because I lied, then fine, but save your almighty bullshit for someone else."

Turning, he sets the beer on my nightstand, and with his insanely muscled arms, he leans over me. I have nowhere to go but back. Above me, his darkened jade eyes stare down at me, his gaze so intense, my body stiffens beneath him.

"You have a lot of nerve speaking to me like that."

Shit, he looks angry, maybe even a little aroused. Fuck, why am I turned on by it? There's something wrong with me. I'm twisted.

Raising my head, I press my lips to his, devouring his mouth with desperate need. Tearing the blanket from my chest, he pulls it back, uncovering my body to below my waist. My hand falls to the bulge in his jeans, and he moans into my mouth. Hand at my breast, he massages it roughly in his large hand, thumbing over the nipple beneath my camisole.

Slipping inside his jeans, I gather his growing cock, the warmth and size of him fills my hand, and I whimper with anticipation.

Another groan fills my mouth as I stroke energetically.

"Fucking woman."

The taste of beer and man are an arousing force as his skilled mouth seduces my mind. I'm lost in the feel of him, the aching need for him.

Pulling back from me, he gathers my arms in his hands, running along my skin before pinning both wrists in one hand. Tracing fingers along the side of my face, his thumb glides over my lips. Dipping into my mouth, I suck at his tip and he hisses, bold green eyes ablaze as he stares down at me.

"There's no going back, Sparrow. Once you're mine, you're mine for good. All you have to do is ask for it." Dominic thrusts against my soaking wet core. "Say it."

Another thrust and my body arches in response, burning with a fire I fear will consume me.

"I want you."

"Be careful what you ask for."

The heat of his lips fuels the scorching fire rising inside me. If I've made a deal with the devil, then I'll be damned. Nothing will ever touch my soul the way Dominic Xavier does.

CHAPTER FOUR

ERIKA

BLINDING light slips through my curtains, and I wince, closing my eyes as I turn away from it. My body aches in more ways than I knew was possible, and what's worse is waking up to an empty bed. Dominic's gone, and the realization leaves a hollow sensation in my chest. Last night I learned a shit too many positions to remember. The culprit for my overly exhausted muscles.

A shower and aspirin. That's my remedy. Easing out of bed, I traipse out of my room and into the shit storm that's our living room. The stench is disgusting. I dodge a used condom and a spilled beer on my way to the bathroom, raising my hand to my mouth in an attempt to keep the vomit at bay. My house has turned into a crime scene with blood on the walls, broken glass, dirty clothes, and an endless supply of butts and empty beer cans. I hate living here.

After a shower, I put on fresh clothes, and rummage

through the disaster of a kitchen and make myself toast and scrape the last of the jam out of the jar. Opening the milk, I take a whiff and gag. Tossing it into the trash, I lean against the refrigerator and close my eyes, wishing this wasn't my life.

The door to my sister's room opens and Ditch stumbles out, his cock half hanging out of his briefs. Gross.

"You should clean this shit up," he barks at me, making his way to our bathroom.

"Don't talk to her like that," Amberlee snaps, ambling out of her room in Ditch's tank and a tiny thong.

"She needs to make herself fucking useful if she isn't going to give ass."

"Shut the fuck up," Amberlee replies, tossing cans and a jacket on the floor as she searches for something.

"E, have you seen my cigarettes?"

The front door pops open after the usual jiggle, and Dori walks in with a grocery bag and a carton of cigarettes.

"Shit, Mom, you're a lifesaver," Amberlee beams.

"Yeah, yeah, you'll owe me."

Dori is unaffected by the mess as she carelessly walks over it, tossing a pack of cigarettes at Amberlee as she passes by.

"I'll be in my room until work tonight. Don't disturb me."

Dori strolls past me without any acknowledgment.

I'm invisible to her, and that's fine with me. Any feelings of love I had for her have been slapped out of me. Over the years, I did my best to stay out of her way, but in her eyes, I'm a waste of room and board, a drain on her miserable existence, and she enjoyed reminding me of it time and time again.

Ditch walks back out of the bathroom, a grimace on his face, making the diamond tattoo at the corner of his eye narrow.

"Why the fuck are you still standing there?"

I can't take this shit.

Stopping in my room, I grab my bag and rush out. Beyond the closing door, I hear Ditch yelling.

"This shit better be cleaned up when I get back."

I go to the one place I can truly have peace, the city library. With their free WiFi, I use their computer to scour the area for jobs. I'll take anything that'll help me get out of my house quicker. The day I got my acceptance letter to community college was a beautiful day, but there's no option to live on campus. I have to stay at home and that realization crushed me. My desperate search brings up a couple results for jobs and I spend the next forty minutes applying to both.

Walking back home, a lump rises in my throat. It's the last place I want to go back to, but I have no money and I need something to eat. The house is silent when I enter, and it's a relief. I avoid the mess all over the floor and start looking through the cabinets. With nothing but crackers and peanut butter I close them and hope to find something in the fridge. Dori's grocery bag has been unpacked. A bundle of bananas and a new loaf of bread sits on the shelf. Maybe she doesn't hate me after all.

I'm just finishing my peanut butter and banana sandwich when Amberlee, Ditch and another Serpent bulldoze through my front door. I don't make it to my bedroom quick enough.

"Why isn't this shit cleaned up?"

I ignore Ditch's comment. "Alee, can I have some money to go to the grocery store?"

Ditch scoffs, separating from Amberlee's hip. "You wanna tell me why you think you can ignore me and parade around here like you're too good to get your hands dirty? Just because Dominic used you for a piece of ass, doesn't mean shit. That's all you were. A good fuck. Maybe now, you can actually make yourself useful." Ditch grips my arm, forcing me to face him. "I'll give you some money, you just need to spread your legs a little."

His tongue whips across his lips and lingers, playing with his lip ring as he stares anticipatively at me. Amberlee shoves him in the back and I glare at her. The bitch told him.

Instinctively, I want to rip my arm from his grasp and slap him, but Dominic's words come to mind. *Use your head, not your knuckles.*

"I'll get the mess cleaned up."

"Now that's more like it." Ditch releases my arm and

grins like he's won the battle.

Amberlee mouths "I'm sorry" as Ditch and the other guy flop onto the couch and turn on the TV.

An hour and a half later, I have all the disgusting trash filled into two black bags and drag them out to the end of the driveway. Returning inside, I'm eager for another shower. Passing the couch, Ditch grabs my arm.

"Order a couple pizzas."

My temper rises a notch, but I remind myself, this is temporary. Play nice to survive. After the order, I disappear into the shower. The warm water relaxes my muscles and washes away the filth. There's a knock at the door, and I jump, startled out of my daze.

"Hurry up, I need in there," Dori grumbles.

Drying and dressing quickly, I leave the bathroom for her to enter. She slips in without another word to me. The doorbell rings and Ditch nods his head to me.

"Get the door."

That request I'm willing to do. That means I can be the first to eat the pizza before everyone's grimy hands paw all over it.

"Bring me a plate and a beer," Ditch orders.

"Get me one too," the other Serpent requests.

Irritated, I set a few slices aside on a plate for me, then gather plates and beers for them. The other Serpent, a guy who looks the same age as Ditch, early to mid-twenties, with a bright blond man bun, winks at me as I hand him his plate and beer.

Don't even start, man bun. Rolling my eyes, I walk

away, and he grabs my wrist, yanking me onto his lap. Putting his plate in my hands, his expression turns arrogant.

"Feed me."

"What?!"

"Drake, are you serious right now?" Amberlee asks in disgust.

"Hell yeah, I am. I want her to feed me. I want you to straddle me as you do it," he says to me, eyes challenging.

Dori walks into the kitchen, takes a look at my plate of pizza, picks it up, and takes it back into her room. My blood is boiling at this point.

"I'm done with this shit."

Pushing off man bun, I head toward the kitchen. Behind me, someone stands. My wrist is yanked, and I'm turned abruptly. "If you know what's good for you, you'll sit on my lap."

Amberlee shoves at Ditch. "That's enough."

Ditch grips her jaw, turning her attention to him. "Watch yourself, Alee."

The light in Amberlee's eyes dim. Mine don't. I knock Drake's hand off my arm. "Fuck off. I'm not sitting on your damn lap and feeding you, you perve."

Drake shoves me onto the couch. "You're gonna do whatever the hell I tell you to."

"Erika, sweet Erika," Ditch laughs behind him. "You should learn your place."

Unbuckling his belt, Drake eyes me viciously. Fear

crawls up my back and takes residence in my body. I move quickly, bolting for the front door. Drake yanks my hair, spinning me around. With a swing as hard as my arm will go, I slam my fist into his face. I don't know where my knuckles hit, but my hand bounces off his face in so much pain, my eyes water. The next several moments are a blur as my adrenaline pumps wildly. Drake swings, backhanding me, and I drop to the floor, the shock trembling my body.

"You little bitch," he seethes between his teeth.

Amberlee's off the couch, screaming. "Leave her alone, you dick."

"All right, all right. Cool it, Drake," Ditch tells him.

Drake licks at his lip, there's a bit of blood. His eyes are ruthless as he stares at me, slowly backing away.

"She has to pay for that, Ditch."

"She will. Just not right now."

I catch the look Ditch gives him, it's a promise. Bile pushes its way up into my throat.

Ditch's gaze switches to me. He pats the couch next to him. "Erika, come're."

Amberlee storms off in search of a cigarette, I assume. Reluctantly, I take the seat next to Ditch, holding my hand to my swollen, throbbing cheek. As I sit down, Ditch puts his arm around me, resting his hand just above my breast. He leans close to my ear.

"We'll get you broke in."

A shiver creeps along my spine. His finger dances across my skin, inching closer to my chest.

"Alee won't always be here to protect you."

My eyes narrow at him, then widen when the front door swings open. Dominic enters, surveys what's in front of him, his eyes darkening, his jaw flexing tightly.

Ditch removes his arm from around me. "Sup, Dom? What are you doin' here?"

"None of your fucking business what I'm doing here. Erika, room, now," he orders.

Shaking, I rush to my room. As soon as I'm behind the closed door, I collapse against my bed, fighting so hard not to cry.

Voices carry an echo into my room, but I can't make out the exact words when my heart is still pumping wildly in my chest. Minutes later, heavy steps lead to my room, and I clam up. Dominic enters my room, sees me on the floor, and lifts me to my feet.

"Ditch says you were all having a good time and things got rough. Now I want you to tell me the truth, all of it. Don't lie to me. Did you fuck him?"

"No! Ditch has been treating me like I'm his bitch all day, ordering me around. I took your advice. I did everything he wanted. I didn't argue. Then Drake wanted me to straddle his lap and feed him. I refused. He shoved me onto the couch and started removing his belt. I ran for the door and he yanked me back. I punched him, then he backhanded me. Ditch told me they'd get me broke in. I know exactly what the fuck he means. If he touches me, I'll cut his damn dick off."

The anger he possesses molds his expression into

the lethal gaze I saw the night he beat up the other Serpent. His boulder muscles tense up. A part of me hopes he goes into the living room and rips Drake and Ditch's throats out. His expression changes when he sees me reach for my head. Feeling woozy, I sit on the edge of my bed.

"What's wrong?" he asks, a hint of worry in his firm tone.

"I haven't eaten much today and I just got smacked around."

"C'mon, we're leaving."

Dominic takes my arm, gently helping me to my feet.

"Where we going?"

"To get you something to eat."

As quickly as my body will allow, I gather shoes, a bag, and jacket. Dominic takes my hand, surprising me. With me in tow, he walks us through the living room. I expect an altercation between him, Ditch, and Drake. Dominic scoffs as we enter the empty living room.

"That's what I fucking thought. Cowards," he grumbles.

"Where'd they go?"

"To run with their tails between their legs."

"You believe me, don't you?"

"Yes," is all he says, tone resounding.

Outside, he stops us in front of his Harley. The royal blue shines against the gleaming silver. He takes care of his bike. That much is obvious. Hopping on, he dips his head for me to climb on behind him. I do, happily, enjoying the feel of his warm body as I wrap my arms around his waist. The engine roars to life, rumbling beneath my legs, vibrating the tension from the day out of my body. I lay my head against his back, feeling safe, relieved to be with him.

I expected a drive-through at McDonald's. Dominic laughed at my surprised reaction when he pulled into a steakhouse. Through dinner, I devoured everything put in front of me, especially since Dominic insisted the meal was on him. Relaxed and sated, I look over the table at him. His colossal arms are folded on the table in front of him. He's a hell of a specimen of a man. The confidence he exudes turns the eyes of every woman he passes, but their gazes don't linger too long. He's equally intimidating and the Serpent jacket no doubt frightens them further.

Tilting his head, he leans back in the booth. "Come sit on my side."

His arm stretches out along the back of the booth as I slide in next to him. Warm fingers graze my damaged cheek and I flinch.

"He hit you hard, didn't he?"

"Looks that bad, huh?"

"Yeah, I don't like seeing your face like this. That shit won't happen again."

Ferocity seeps through his voice and it turns me on hearing it. I think dangerous Dominic likes me a little bit.

"I'm glad you came over when you did. I was happy to see you for multiple reasons," I share, leaning my head against his arm.

"I came to see you. I wanted you to ride me before I took you out to dinner. I'm not thrilled my plans were interrupted."

"You were coming over to take me on a date?" I beam.

Dominic's mouth curves. "Something like that."

"You like me, don't you?"

With his hand on my back, he slides me closer. "I'm still deciding."

"Now who's lying," I tease.

A chuckle slips through his lips as he gives me a side glance.

"You're cute, Sparrow. Real cute," he counters.

I giggle and nuzzle up against him. His arm rests on my back, warming my body.

"You ready to head back?"

A frown tugs at my lips. "You mean home?"

"Yeah, I have business to take care of, but I'll be back later."

"Can you take me with you? I'll stay out of the way."

Dominic studies my face. His brows narrow in thought. "It's club business. You can't be around. I'll come back later," he promises.

His tone brooks no argument, so I don't push it. "Thank you for dinner and for coming to see me. If you hurry your ass back, I'll make it worth your while," I wink.

Dominic's hand clasps the back of my neck. Leaning to my ear, he whispers, "I know you will, baby. I'm anxious to feel that tight pussy around my cock as much as you are."

With a kiss to my cheek, he releases his grip on me.

"Now let's get moving so I can get shit taken care of."

The brush of his warm lips and wicked words instantly light the fire that burns for him. I'm eager for him to return from his business. When I'm with him, I feel like an actual person, like I actually give a damn, rather than the trash everyone else treats me as.

Pulling up the drive, there are two other motorcycles sitting in the driveway. I recognize one of them—Ditch's and my stomach coils.

Dominic takes my hand, walking us inside. A grey cloud of fog greets us as we enter followed by the sound of grunting and two people slapping together just beyond Amberlee's bedroom door. Dominic takes me with him, busting through the door without a care. On the bed, Ditch has Amberlee bent over, fucking her from behind as her mouth slides up and down Drake's dick.

"What the fuck, Dom?"

"Finish up and get your asses out here," Dominic orders.

Dominic takes a seat on the couch and pulls me into

his lap. I'm still stunned at what I just saw. Dominic places his fingers on my jaw, turning my face to his.

"You all right?"

"Yeah, I just—"

"Saw your sister getting double penetrated."

My stomach churns. "Yeah."

Dominic laughs. "I've seen worse."

"With her?" I question, my voice elevated.

"Yeah. Your sister's a slut. But you two aren't anything alike, are you?"

"No," I reply adamantly.

"That's good. I won't have my girl touched by anyone else but me, *ever*."

The words *my girl* linger in my head, thrilling me.

"What the fuck? What do you want?" Ditch snaps, hitching his pants over his hips as he walks out the door.

Drake follows behind, zipping his fly, and Dominic's eyes narrow to slits. I see a predator in his gaze. I know it's wrong, but I'm glad to see that look directed toward Drake.

"Drake, you're joining me on a run. We're leaving now. Ditch, I'm leaving Erika in your care. Anything happens to her while I'm gone and I'll hold your ass responsible," he emphasizes the word responsible and Ditch's eye twitches.

"She yours now?" His tongue darts out, playing with his lip ring. I can't read his expression, but there's something about it that sends chills up my back.

"Exactly what that fucking means. Let's go, Drake."

Dominic squeezes my ass, indicating I need to stand. When we do, he clutches my neck and hair, pulling me to him. His kiss is aggressive, provocative. I feel like it's for a show as much as it's for pleasure.

"See you later."

His thumb grazes my cheek, a brief gesture of affection. My body responds, tingling all over.

The moment Dominic and Drake walk out the door, I head toward my room. Ditch blocks my path.

"You think you're hot shit because Dom likes fucking your cunt? It won't last, little sister, and when he's had his fill, he'll toss you aside without a care, but don't worry, I'll take *real good* care of you after that."

My teeth clench as his hand caresses my arm. Amberlee walks out of her room, and Ditch winks, leering at me.

"What are you two talking about?" she asks, irritated.

Ditch's devilish gaze peels off my face and looks to Amberlee. "Just welcoming her to the crew. She's Dom's property now."

I shove past him, my shoulder hitting his as I force my way to my room. Slamming it behind me, I lean against the door, taking several slow deep breaths.

The door pushes open and I move, letting Amberlee in. She looks me over, her eyes lingering on my damaged cheek before squinting away from it. "You know what that means? Being Dom's property?"

"What?"

"That means you don't ever lie to him or betray him. You belong to him and do whatever he wants. This is why I warned you about sleeping with him. He owns you now, and there isn't shit I can do about it, so don't ever piss him off because I can't protect you if you do."

"I'm not property. I'm a fucking person."

Amberlee shakes her head. Her wavy, short, red hair swishes back and forth. "You're so fucking naive. The Serpents, they kill people, they do whatever the hell they want without a care for the law. These aren't your high school bad boys, E. They're animals. So do yourself a favor and keep Dom satisfied."

CHAPTER FIVE

ERIKA

THE PARTY HAS STARTED and Dom still hasn't returned. Sitting up in my bed, I have my knee bent and a book leaning against it in my hand. I've read the same paragraph a few times. Realizing that, I pull my attention from it and stare off in thought as the music thumps in heavy drum beats. From the sounds of it, this party is wilder than last night's. A headache forms at the thought. That's more mess I'm sure Ditch will insist I clean up. That guy is a serious problem. One I'd desperately like to be rid of. What the hell Amberlee sees in him, I don't understand.

My bedroom door opens and my attention is drawn to Amberlee in her black leather skinny pants and red tank top with side boob popping out. Her hair is curled and her make-up fresh, but it doesn't completely hide the harsh bruising I see trimming her jawline. Yet she enters my room with a congenial smile.

With two drinks in each hand, she joins me on the bed, handing one cup to me.

"I thought we could have some sister time. I can do your hair and make-up. Help you pick out something hot to wear."

Taking the cup from her hand, I swallow down the mixed drink she's made. The taste of orange juice and vodka is bold as it flows down my throat.

"What happened to your face?"

Amberlee takes a sip of her drink. "Ditch and I got into a fight."

"When? I didn't hear you guys."

Amberlee swings her legs, lying flat on her stomach with her ankles crossed behind her.

"It was before you and Dom got back."

"What'd you fight about?"

"Stupid shit."

She's evading. I can see it in her golden hazel eyes.

"Was it about me?"

"Part of it."

With another swig of my drink, my lips pull down as my expression morphs reflecting my sympathy.

"You really shouldn't be with a guy who thinks it's ok to hit a woman."

"Please don't," Amberlee scoffs, her eyes rolling. "I want tonight to be fun."

I finish off my drink and set it on the nightstand. "Fine, I won't say anything, but I'm sure you know what I'm trying to say...you deserve better."

"I'm sorry Drake hit you. That got out of hand quickly. He's a real ass."

Without thinking about it, I rub my cheek.

Amberlee pops upright. "Let's cover that up. I'll make you look really pretty...well, prettier than you already are."

Her cheery attitude about my makeover is hard to decline. "All right. Don't do anything bold. Keep it light."

"Yeah, yeah."

Amberlee crosses my room to my vanity and rummages through my makeup box. With a satisfied selection of products, she pats the chair for me to fill. Twenty minutes later, my makeup is done, and she's almost finished putting loose curls in my long, auburn hair. Looking in the mirror, I'm impressed with how good a job she did with my makeup. The smoky eyes she gave me aren't too bold, thankfully, and accentuate my eyes, making them pop. I have a feeling Dominic is going to like what he sees.

"You're really good at this. It sucks you got fired from Mane Attraction."

"I know, I kinda miss working there."

Through the mirror, I can see the regret in her eyes.

"I'd give Roger a freebie if he'd give me my job back, but Ditch would flip the fuck out if he found out."

"So he doesn't care about sharing you, but it has to be on his terms?"

"Yeah, he's all about sharing me with whoever the fuck he wants," she replies, her tone toxic.

"Was that the other part of the fight?"

Amberlee sets the curling rod on the table and quickly unplugs it.

"I need another drink. I'll get you one too."

Amberlee disappears with our cups and I pick out something sexy, but not too revealing to wear.

Walking back in, Amberlee looks over my knee high grey boots, cream, off-the-shoulder, sweater dress, and the long, gold necklace with the wing charm at the end.

"You look hot," she grins, handing me my drink.

With a short-lived giggle, I enjoy the fruity flavor of the drink as I swallow it down.

"Thanks for making me pretty."

"You're always pretty even when you're in pjs and a messy bun. It's why I have to work so hard to keep the guys off you."

The liquor from the first drink has taken effect. Warmth is spreading throughout my body and I'm feeling giggly.

"What do you mean? They always want to fuck you, not me."

Amberlee rolls her eyes. "That's because I put out and they knew you wouldn't."

"Yeah, well, I didn't want any of the guys who only wanted me if I'd put out."

Amberlee chugs the last of her drink. "You always were the smart one."

She takes my cup after I finish off the last of it. Nodding to the party, she wraps a hand through my arm. "Let's join the party. It'll be nice to have my sister there for a change."

Outside my door is a whole other world. Amberlee pulls me into it and I take in the crowd. There's a lot of Serpents in our living room tonight. Every surface is covered with an ass or two. There's a cooler in the corner overflowing with beer cans. Part of the kitchen counter is completely covered in liquor bottles. The scent of sex and marijuana is already heavy in the air.

There are a few new women I haven't seen before, hanging on their men like Christmas lights on a tree. As Amberlee tugs me along, the glares I receive from them are lethal. Little do they know I have no interest in any of their men. Only one man has my interest and I'm anxiously waiting for him to arrive.

Ditch turns his attention as Amberlee wraps an arm around him. In his peripheral, he sees me. Fully turning his head, he gives me a once over. With a twitchy hand, he rubs his thumb under his lip. His gaze is frozen on me, snaking up my legs to my chest, and it's making me uncomfortable. Amberlee nudges him, and he laughs it off, leans in, and kisses her.

"She looks good, babe. You did good."

"Fuck yeah, I did. She looks gorgeous."

Ditch shoves a drink into my hand. "Now maybe you can loosen up and not be such a bitch tonight."

"Can you try to be nice?" Amberlee asks, irritation evident in her tone.

"Sure, babe, but you'll have to make it up to me later." Ditch's smile is devious. Fuck, I hate this guy.

Amberlee reaches between his legs. "I know just how you like it."

Their lips lock in a disgusting show of passion and I bolt to the kitchen. Dumping the drink Ditch gave me in the sink, I reach for a new cup and make my own drink. As I'm pouring I begin to feel odd. I'm incredibly warm, warmer than alcohol usually makes me. The hand holding the vodka bottle is shaking slightly. I set the bottle down and focus on my senses. The colors around me seem brighter, the scents stronger. Raising my hand in front of my face, I stare at it, noticing the fine details and lines of my skin. Wiggling my fingers, I giggle. An overwhelming euphoric sensation overtakes me, completely relaxing my body.

Glancing across the room, I see Amberlee watching me. She winks at me, then heads my direction.

"I feel amazing. What the hell is going on?"

Amberlee rubs my arm and the contact makes me purr with pleasure. My eyes pinch closed. "God, that feels so good."

Amberlee moves up my arm and rubs along my naked shoulder and neck.

A low purr slips from my parted lips. "What's going on? Why does that feel so damn good?"

"It's ecstasy. You're high."

My eyes jolt open. "You put it in my drink?"

"Yeah, it'll loosen you up for tonight."

She keeps rubbing and any anger I start to feel is eased away by the pleasurable sensations of her massage.

"Why did you spike my drink?"

"You like it, don't you?"

"Yeah," I giggle.

"I knew you would. Let's go into the bathroom. It'll be a whole other experience."

Amberlee takes my hand and I immediately notice how soft her skin is. I rub my thumb along it, fascinated by the feel of it. Pulling me into the bathroom, she flicks on the light and closes the door behind us. The light is gloriously bright. She positions me in front of the mirror and I look at myself. It's incredible. I don't recognize me. My pupils are huge, almost filling my irises. My skin is golden, my eyes intricate with designs and lines darting out from my expanded pupils. My makeup is shiny, and I get lost admiring the sparkles.

Touching my left arm, I slowly run my fingers along my skin, and that single movement causes goose bumps. I close my eyes, reveling in the sensations I feel everywhere I touch.

"Wow, Alee, this is incredible."

Fingers grazing along my waist, she dips her hands lower and squeezes my hips. "Wait til you fuck Dominic. The feeling will blow your mind." Still holding me, she kisses my cheek. "Let's join the party."

Just the thought of Dominic filling me makes me grin. Amberlee takes my hand and leads me back to the crowd. The music is thumping. Each beat reaching into the depths of my chest. Every sound is more acute, every person, every color utterly spellbinding. My eyes wander over the room, studying everything, taking it all in. My eyes whip back to the front door as it opens and my body instantly tingles with excitement and desire.

Dominic and Drake enter farther into the room and I watch him like a cat slowly hunting her prey. Drake steps out from behind Dominic and I immediately notice Drake's black eye and bowed head. My lip curls in satisfaction. I hope it hurt like a bitch when Dominic hit him, at least that's what I'm hoping happened. Glancing at Dominic's knuckles, I'm assured my thoughts were correct.

My lip slides from between my teeth as Dominic's eyes catch me across the living room. A forefinger and thumb wipe over his mouth and chin. He stops where he's at and watches my movements as I saunter toward him. His gaze is carnal as he looks me over from my boot heels to my eyes. His sensual gaze says it all. The intensity is rich and beneath them, I know what he's thinking. It's the same thing I am. I want his cock buried deep inside me, filling me, lighting my body on fire.

My hands slip beneath his jacket, gliding up his shirt, fisting it as I reach his chest. Pulling him down to me, I ravage his mouth. Hands cupping my ass, he squeezes as his tongue intertwines with mine. Against my body, his body is warm, delicious, hard, and I want him naked in all his glory. His hand snakes up my back, fisting my hair, pulling my head back to look at him. His gaze is ravenous. I'm putty in his hands, and he knows it. His gorgeous green eyes amaze me. I stare at the lines and details, fascinated by how elaborate and stunning they are.

"What are you high on?"

"Ecstasy, Alee spiked my drink."

A grumble rolls out of his chest. "Is it your first time?"

"Yes," I purr, rubbing my hands beneath his shirt. The touch of his hard abs making me aroused.

"Look who's back," Ditch announces to the crowd. "We've been anxiously waiting for you, Dom. Tonight's a perfect night to initiate your new girl."

My head is fuzzy with desire, but I catch the word *initiate*.

Dominic kisses my head, still holding me close. "Fucking bastard," he mutters under his breath.

The crowd around us moves back, leaving us just off center of the living room.

"We'll give you some time to prepare her, but don't take long. We're eager for the show." Ditch's lowered head and darkened eyes dim my enchanting high.

Dominic slides his hand around my arm and leads me to my room. Closing it, he pulls me to him. Moments ago, I wanted us here with my arms and legs wrapped around him and him carrying me to my bed. Now, my head hurts as my incredible high fights with my combusting nerves.

"What's he talking about?" I ask, panicked.

"Did you get dressed up for me?" he asks, massaging my back.

"Yes." My eyes close shut as I indulge in his intoxicating touch.

His hands continue down my back, slowly, methodically, applying just the right pressure. Bringing one hand around to the front, he slides his hand between my legs. Forcing my panties to the side, he slides a finger into me, and I gasp a quickened breath. My head falls back as I'm lost to the rush of heat coursing through my body. My grip tightens, fisting his shirt.

"Dominic, I want you so bad."

He leans his head next to my ear, his breath sending waves of pleasure over my neck and shoulders. "You look sexy as fuck. I wanna eat your pussy and watch you cum as I pound into your tight hole."

My mouth elicits several whimpers as he adds another finger and quickens his pace, finger fucking me deep.

"What are you waiting for?"

"We're gonna do it...out there."

My eyes shoot open and I pull back from him. "What?"

He cuts the space between us, holding me against

him. I feel the enlarged bulge in his jeans and it's a struggle not to grind against it.

"What do you mean, out there?"

"Do you want to be with me?" he asks, his tone serious. I watch the shift in his gaze as he awaits my answer.

"Yes."

"Then it's required you go through an initiation."

"You mean I have to have sex with you...in front of everyone?"

I sway, feeling woozy. Dominic's grip tightens, holding me steady.

"You going to be sick?"

"No, I'm freaking out."

Dominic puts his hand on my chin and directs my face to look up at him. "Don't think about anyone else. Focus on me. Focus on how good it feels to have me inside you."

"Will anyone touch me?" The thought revolts me.

Dominic's brows dip inward, his eyes darken. "Fuck no. They touch you and I'll gut them where they stand."

I release the breath I was holding.

"Do I have to get completely naked?"

"Don't worry about that. Just focus on us."

"What would've happened if I said no?"

Dominic touches my face, caressing his thumb over my cheek. "You don't want to know." Leaning down, he kisses me, drawing my lustful desires to the surface. "It's gonna be fine," he assures me. "I'll get you a drink. Settle those nerves."

"We don't have to walk out there and start fucking?"

His mouth curves into a delicious smile as he lets out an amused laugh. "No. We can go out and drink and relax. I'm not gonna rush you. They can wait til we're ready."

Wrapping his arms around me, he rests them on my lower back, rubbing along my ass and back.

"You look fucking beautiful. It means something to me that you got dressed up like this."

"Yeah?"

His thumb pulls at my lip. I suck the tip and he leans in, sucking and kissing my neck.

"It does and makes me want to take you hard."

My body tingles and my head clouds, pushing out any nervous thoughts. His hand slides between my legs, rubbing my underwear against my clit.

"I'm having a hard time not taking you now."

My head rests on his chest as I moan. "I'm becoming addicted to your touch."

Dominic cups my pussy, kissing me deep and rough. As he pulls away, I bring my fingers to my tingling lips.

"That's good. That's what I want."

He takes my hand, leading me out of the room. My head is still in a daze, but nerves splinter through my body when several gazes in the crowd look toward us. Dominic makes eye contact with Amberlee and tilts his head, indicating she needs to join us. Taking us into the kitchen, he grabs a whiskey bottle and takes two long swigs, then sets it down. Amberlee walks into the kitchen and he folds his arms, leaning against the counter, his muscles bulge, his gaze menacing.

"Don't give her any drugs without my permission. I'll let it slide tonight because I know why you did it." He puts his palm out, curling his fingers in, then out. "Give me three of your E."

Reaching into the pocket of her leather pants, she pulls out a small plastic bag with a lot of tiny blue pills in it. Opening it, she pulls out three of them and places them in Dominic's palm.

"Anything else?" she asks, her tone mocking.

Dominic reaches out, cupping her jaw and cheek. "I see he's left his mark again." He drops his hand, taking mine. "When you gonna realize you don't deserve that shit?"

"We done here?"

Dominic shakes his head, the disappointment evident. "Yeah, we're done."

She turns to leave and he calls her name. She looks back at him, expectantly.

"Thanks for looking after her," he says with a nod.

Lifting her chin, acknowledging, she walks off to rejoin Ditch and the Serpents he's drinking with.

Moving me in front of him, he places me between his legs. "Open your mouth."

I do and he places a pill on the tip of my tongue.

"This will be your last one tonight. I want you to enjoy it."

Without a need for a drink, I swallow it down. Dominic pops the other two pills in his mouth and chases them with another drink of whiskey. Clasping his hand at my neck, his fingers tangle in my hair as he brings me to him. Slipping his tongue between my lips, he kisses me deep, moving his hands all over my body, hugging me to him as his mouth speaks for him, illustrating how much he wants me.

Snaking up the inside of my dress, his hand finds the strap of my underwear. He pulls at the strap, then matches his hand on the opposite side, tugging them off my hips. Bringing them down my legs, he has me step out of them.

Shoving the material in his pocket, he winks, "You won't be needing those."

I freely fall forward into his arms, giggling, "I'm glad you're here. You make everything better."

He kisses me again, then steps away from the counter, taking me with him. "C'mon."

On the way to the living room, he grabs a beer. Before sitting down, he sheds his Serpent jacket and t-shirt, tossing them on the back of the loveseat, leaving his abs and ink gloriously on display. Dropping down, he pulls me onto his lap. Lifting the beer, he opens it and takes a drink.

My eyes roam the living room, and my gaze lands on

Drake, getting handsy with a blonde. He sees me looking and I smirk. I can't help myself.

"Did you hit him?" I ask.

"Yeah, he won't be touching you again. You can be sure of that."

"Why does everyone take orders from you?"

Dominic rubs my back, and I momentarily close my eyes, taking pleasure in the sensation it causes.

"A couple reasons. We have a rank in the club. I'm the second in command. I don't take orders from anyone, but Christian, and even then, only if I'm willing to." He pulls me closer, within a whisper. "And the other is they're afraid of me."

Tracing my finger over his ink, I admire how detailed and beautiful each tattoo is.

"Why are they afraid of you?"

"Can you handle the answer?"

"Yes."

"I'm willing to get blood on my hands."

"You mean you're willing to kill another man?"

Setting the beer on the stand next to the loveseat, he adjusts the way I'm sitting, making me straddle his lap.

"Yes."

"Have you...killed another man before?"

Looking at his striking features I notice his dilated pupils. With his hands on my hips, he moves forward and back over his growing erection. I push into him, wanting to feel him better. Letting out a quiet moan, he reaches down, unbuttoning his jeans.

"We'll talk about that later."

I'm brought forward, his mouth taking mine with an intense need. Every movement spikes my growing high. I'm blazing with heat, my core soaking wet. I hunger for more of his touch. Losing myself to the thundering music and exquisite desire coursing through me, I pull his erection from his open jeans and briefs. Raising my ass, I slide down on top of him. His head falls back. "Fuck."

Fierce, lascivious gaze meeting mine, he slips his hands beneath my dress, raising it over my head and off. It flutters to the floor somewhere behind me.

With whispered words, he warms my ear. "Fuck me, my beautiful Sparrow."

Desire, rich and sweet, urges my ravenous need for him. Arms around his neck, my head to his, he grips my hips as I ride him.

"Yes, baby, just like that."

Just like the beat of the music, we fall into a rhythm. Moans echoing from my parted lips, he smothers my cries, swirling his tongue around mine.

Behind me, my bra unclasps. With a sensual caress, he slides the straps from my arms and tosses it.

Hoots and hollers are an echo around us. It's the first I've become aware of anyone's presence. Keeping my gaze hostage to his, I never look away. He's the only thing that matters, and I'm in too deep, drowning in his touch, to care about anything else.

We're a blazing inferno of heat as he holds my back, supporting me as I thrust fast and hard against his cock.

Wrapping my hair around his fist, he pulls my head back, sucking my nipple into his mouth as I continue to writhe over him. Filling my free breast in his hand, he massages it, thumbing over the nipple. A wet, slick heat travels up the center of my breasts as he licks across my skin, then switches to my other nipple, sucking it between his teeth and letting it pop free.

Gripping my hips, he slides his ass closer to the edge. Leaning back, he places my arms above my head, onto the top of the chair. With a controlled hold on my hips, he thrusts up, repeatedly pounding me on his cock.

Crying out, I moan through my release. Trembling, I whimper through the aftershocks as Dominic thickens and pumps into me. Pulling me to him, my head rests against his before he kisses me.

"Fuck, that was good."

Reaching between my legs, he swirls against my clit, and I hiss in a breath. Putting his middle finger against my lips, I suck to the base, tasting myself on his finger.

"Now I'm gonna fuck something else."

Dominic stands, my legs still wrapped around him. Touching my ass, he prods the tight hole as he carries me to my room.

CHAPTER SIX

ERIKA

On all fours, I look over my shoulder as the bed dips from Dominic's weight. Between his hands, he squeezes a bottle of lubricant he retrieved from Amberlee's room. My body is humming with electricity, still riding my high, sensitive to every touch. Dominic spreads my ass cheeks, circling my puckered hole.

"I'm already getting worked up thinking about fucking your ass."

His finger fills my entrance, and I grip the sheets beneath me.

"How's that feel?" he asks, slowly sliding in and out, the sensation driving me wild.

"So good."

"Fuck," a low groan rolls out from his chest. "I knew you'd like this. You want my cock in your ass, don't you?"

"Yes."

Another finger stretches me, and I wince before his pace picks up, pleasuring my ass. A third finger and the pleasure mixes with pain. Hand on my shoulder, he massages his thumb into my muscles, relaxing me as he stretches me, readying me to take him.

"The way you came for me out there..." his voice is low, a tenor riveted with sexuality, "It was the hottest thing I've ever seen."

Withdrawing his fingers, I hear the slick sound of the lubricant as he strokes along his erection. Pulling my ass cheeks apart, he presses his head to my hole.

"Relax your body. I want you to enjoy this."

The pressure builds as his head pushes in. I try hard to stay relaxed, but he's so big, the pressure is overwhelming.

"Dom, it hurts," I grimace, fisting the sheets.

Rubbing his hand over my back, he massages, kneading his strong hand into my muscles as his other hand wraps around my hip, sliding between my legs. Heat builds at my core. Every touch, every stroke, the feel of his hands on my body eases the strain on my backside. With each caress along my back, he eases further in. Pulling out some, there's a release of pressure and with the next thrust, it switches to pleasure.

"Oh, God, Dom. That feels so good."

"I knew you could take all of me," his voice is husky, low, followed by a satisfied groan.

"Your ass feels even better than your pussy."

My ass is tugged, slapping against his pelvis, as he

thrusts deep and hard, filling me completely. Having him take me like this is an overpowering sensation. I feel vulnerable, desired, closer to him than before. The rush of pleasure that washes over my body with each thrust of his cock forces uncontrollable moans from my lips.

His own moans echo through my room as he continues to pound into me, slamming me onto him.

"You're trembling. You gonna cum for me?"

"Yes," I cry out.

Like a force of nature, I'm consumed by pleasure. A euphoric sensation so strong, it blurs my vision, obliterating my senses. My arms give out, and I drop, my head touching the bed as I writhe and moan through each pulse of utter bliss tearing through me.

An explicit groan escapes from his chest as he pulls my ass tight against him, thickening and releasing into me. Beneath me, an arm gathers me, putting me upright, holding my back to his chest as I pant through each breath. Hand around my throat, the other slides between my legs, gathering at my slick wetness, twirling around my clit, teetering me on the edge of another orgasm.

"Knowing no other man has had you, that you're all mine, it does things to me. Turns me on in a way I've never felt. You're better than a ride or a drug. You're pure freedom, Sparrow."

Laying in Dominic's arms, I close my eyes as his hand caresses along my side, raising goosebumps on my skin. Looking into his eyes, I feel myself getting lost in the depths of his stunning green irises and the mysterious man behind them.

"I want to know everything about you."

Touching my face, he caresses my hair and cheek. "Not everything. There are things I don't want you to know. Things I don't want you to see. My life is dark and dangerous. I don't want you part of that. With all the shit I deal with, you're my only escape from it. The only good thing that isn't tainted."

His dilated pupils tell me he's still enjoying his high. My fingertip follows a trail of ink, and he stops caressing me, indulging in my touch.

"Tell me what you will."

"I had to grow up fast, just like you. Home life was rough. I saw shit at too young of an age. My father and uncle were Serpents, so it's no surprise I was drawn into this kind of life. The first time I killed a man was when I was seventeen. My brother was older than me, but he was weak, lacked self-control, a lot like your sister. He'd gotten addicted to heroin, was making bad decisions to get a fix. A deal went wrong, he'd stolen some shit he was supposed to sell. I was with him, along with a couple other Serpents when a gun was pulled on him. His head wasn't right and he got himself shot. I tried to get to him, to put him on my bike. I remember seeing the blood pooling on the ground. I was scared he was going to die. Reaching for him, I felt a shooting pain in my side." He adjusts the way he's lying to reveal a one-inch scar blended in his tattoos. "I was stabbed. My choice was kill the owner of the knife or lay in a pool of blood next to my brother. You know what happened next."

Dominic doesn't flinch as I thumb over the uneven skin. "What happened to your brother?"

"He didn't make it."

"I'm sorry."

Turning toward me, he grazes a finger over my jaw. "You have nothing to be sorry for. My brother did it to himself. He was weak. I know that sounds cold, but as a Serpent, you can't be weak."

Taking hold of his massive bicep, I scoot closer to him. His arm folds around me.

"I think Ditch is weak. I see him snorting cocaine too often and he's easily angered by stupid things. I recently heard Alee yelling at him about not being able to get an erection."

Dominic leans back, raising my chin to him. "Erika, don't ever say that to him or anyone else. Promise me, now."

"I won't," I assure him.

"He'd lose his mind if you emasculated him in front of anyone. He'd hurt you and I'd have to kill him."

"Would you...kill him?"

With a languid motion, his finger trails up my inner thigh, across my opening.

"If he tried to take what was mine, I would."

My lips part, my breath escaping as he toys with my clit.

"Would you be telling me these things if you weren't high right now?"

Laughing quietly, his gaze raises to my face. "No, I'm not one to share things about myself, but I'm high as a kite and wanting to confess all my sins to you."

"How long were you watching me before the night we kissed?"

"Part your legs for me," he instructs, his eyes glistening with a renewed hunger.

Lying more on my back, I open them for him to explore.

"How long?"

Fingers sliding into my opening, my breath catches, and a proud smile spreads his lips.

"About three weeks. You caught my attention from the first moment I saw you, but when you avoided the parties, drinking, drugs, fucking any of my brothers that's when my curiosity grew. The night you stood your ground with Tex, I saw the fighter in you. I wanted you then like I do now."

Adding another finger, he works my hole making me drenched with need.

"How do you want me?"

"Wet, baby, always wet and ready for me."

Rolling on top of me, he takes my arms, pinning them down above my head. Bending my knees toward my chest, I give him better access. With one powerful thrust, he fills me, pulls back and thrusts deeper, harder.

With my arms pinned, he has total control, and I love it. This is exactly how I imagined him dominating me, taking me with such raw passion.

"You like it when I take control of you, don't you?" he asks, thrusting hard, his head hitting my cervix.

Arching my back, my body and mind plunge into an erotic euphoria.

"Tell me how much you love my cock in you."

Another hard thrust, the rapture pushes me over the edge. My release shakes my body. I quiver beneath him, and he pulls out, stroking his cock as warm cum jets across my stomach.

Firmly caressing my thighs, his eyes are glossy as he looks me over.

"I like seeing my cum all over you."

"Marking your territory?" I tease.

"Damn straight. You're mine. Every part of you, whenever I want, however I want."

His eyes are challenging, testing me.

Sitting up, I pull his face to me. "I wouldn't have agreed to the initiation if I didn't already feel that way."

When his lips cover mine, the kiss is heated, passionate, a seal of approval.

Grabbing a towel from my laundry basket, he cleans me off. With the towel tossed back in the basket, I crawl into his open arms. Pulling the blanket over us, I lay on his chest, his strong arm holding me affectionately. Thumb grazing across my skin, I drift into a relaxed sleep.

WARM LIGHT TOUCHES MY FACE, and I blink twice, my head throbbing behind my temples. Reaching over, expecting the bed cold and empty, my hand finds Dominic's warm chest, and I'm surprised as much as I am elated.

Stirring awake, he turns to his side, pulling me flush against him.

"I'm glad you didn't leave."

"After the show we put on last night, there was no way in hell I was leaving you alone."

Pinching my eyes closed, I try to deal with the ache in my head and stomach. "I feel miserable. My head is killing me."

"I know." Dominic rubs at the base of my neck. "Coming off that shit is rough. We'll get out of here and get breakfast."

"I'll get us some water."

Finding fresh clothes, I amble toward the kitchen, avoiding the usual mess on the way. I'm surprised to see a couple Serpents still here, passed out on the furniture. I creep to the bathroom, trying not to wake them. Nearing the door, I hear a woman's plea, begging for someone to stop. Her words are raspy as if her breath is being choked out of her. Turning the knob, a crack of light seeps through before I see the terrifying scene.

Drake has his belt wrapped around the blond woman's throat I saw last night. He's pulling tight, her throat red and raw as he pounds into her from behind. His eyes meet mine in the mirror and his expression morphs, becoming menacing, slamming into her harder, never taking his dangerous glare from the mirror. Closing the door, I run back to Dominic.

Shutting the door behind me, I rush to the bed, falling on top of his chest in a panic.

"Drake is hurting a woman in my bathroom. I think he's raping her. You need to do something."

With an arm lazily draped over his head, he strokes my side and shuts his eyes. "Drake has fetishes. He likes to hurt women when he fucks them."

He blows me off, and I rise from the bed, anger building in me.

"This is my house, Dom. I'm not putting up with shit like that."

Storming to the door, Dominic moves out of my bed like lightning, pushing my door shut before I can walk through it.

"I'm sorry. This isn't your house anymore."

"What do you mean?"

"Christian owns it. He's the landlord now."

"How the hell did this happen?"

"It's one of the things we do as Serpents. We own a lot of properties and they serve different purposes."

"What purpose does my house serve?"

"It's one of the things I want you kept away from, so don't ask details."

"Amberlee said I wasn't part of the deal. What deal, Dom?"

Dominic pulls me closer, stroking my face in an attempt to cool my anger. I shove his hand away and his eyes darken.

Anger surges through me, clenching my jaw. "What deal?"

Pressing me against the bed frame, he moves in closer, his posture dominating. "Don't ever shove me away like that when I'm trying to comfort you."

"I...want...them...out," I seethe. "If you won't help me, fine. I'll do it on my own."

Slipping out through the gap between him and the bed, I yank my door open and storm toward the living room. Boulder-like arms wrap around my waist, easily lifting me off the floor. I'm quickly brought back into my room, the door slamming behind us. Squirming in his arms, I try to break free.

Against my ear, his voice is low, controlled. "Don't fight me, Sparrow. I never want to hurt you, but I can easily overpower you and accidentally hurt you, so stop, *now*."

My body goes limp in his arms. He releases me, turning me to face him. Dark, jade green eyes study my expression.

"Why are you so angry?"

"I hate living here. I hate Ditch and Drake. I hate having no control over my own life. I'm trapped here and I don't even know what the hell is going on."

Hands on my hips, he pulls me to him. This time I don't fight him, he's taken it out of me. When my body complies, his expression softens.

"Do you trust me?"

Placing my hands on his naked torso, I rub along his hardened abs. "Completely."

"Then know that whatever is going on, it's safer you don't know. The more knowledge you have, the more danger you're in."

"I'm not blind to my surroundings. I know the Serpents deal drugs."

With a stroke of his hand, he runs his fingers through my hair, moving it off my face.

"You've seen the Serpents using drugs. You haven't seen any drug deals, have you?"

Pausing, I think over his words. He's right. I haven't seen drug deals. It's always been an assumption.

"No, I haven't."

His fingers brush over my jaw, then cup my chin, raising my mouth to his.

"Let's get out of here. I wanna spend the day with you."

"You're walking me to the bathroom first. I need to get cleaned up and *don't* want to run into Drake again."

Moving to the bed, he gathers the rest of his clothes.

"We'll take a shower at my house after I pick you up a few things."

"A few things?"

"Whatever products you need and we'll get you a morning-after pill."

"Fuck." Last night comes rushing back to me. "We didn't use protection and you didn't pull out."

Sliding his dark, worn-in jeans over his briefs, he buttons them. "We were completely lost in the moment."

My body tingles from the memories. Last night was incredible and I didn't even notice a single person around us.

Watching me, Dominic's lip slips from between his teeth. "You're getting hot thinking about it, aren't you?"

My mouth curves into a flirtatious grin. "I am." Stepping to him, I place my hands on his chest, rubbing down to his abs. "I can't help it. You do it to me."

Tongue pushed against mine, he possessively claims my mouth.

"You do the same to me."

Wrapping my arms around his back, I massage his muscles.

"Last night was about claiming me in front of everyone, wasn't it?"

With his hand on the side of my face, he nods. "Everyone knows now. You're my woman. It'll give you added protection. No Serpent will touch you."

That statement relieves tension and worry I had buried deep.

"You looked beautiful riding me like you did. No doubt every one of my brothers wanted you."

"They can't have me. I'm all yours."

"Don't forget it." Scooping me up, I wrap my legs around his waist as he nuzzles his face into my neck, licking and sucking me, making me laugh when his scruff tickles me.

"I want to hear that laugh more often."

I lean back in his arms, admiring his masculine features and strong jawline.

"I don't even remember the last time I laughed out of pure happiness. It feels good."

Setting me down by my closet, he pecks my cheek.

"Pack what you need. I'm heading to take a piss."

Dominic leaves and I grab a duffle, filling it with anything I might need for today and a potential stay over. My door opens and it's not Dominic like I expected. Amberlee strolls in. Her hair pulled back in a tiny ponytail.

"You hate me?"

I glance at her and frown, then continue packing. "Of course, I don't hate you. I know why you spiked my drink with ecstasy, and honestly, I appreciate it."

Relief washes over her sharp features. "I overheard Ditch talking with another Serpent about forcing Dom to claim you and for you to put out. I had to go through it too, but no one prepared me. I didn't want you to go through that embarrassment. You're lucky to have Dom. He really cares about you." There's a sadness in her tone and it tugs at my heart.

"You could have the same. Dump his ass."

"It's not that easy. Imagine if you wanted to break it off with Dom. How do you think he'd handle it?"

If he's anywhere as hooked as I am, he'd flip. I know it.

"So, when you're with a Serpent, there's no walking away?"

Amberlee's eyes moisten as she shakes her head. "Not unless he wants to end it. If I tried, I'd be humiliating him in front of his brothers. He'd hurt me for it."

"I can talk to Dom. Maybe he can talk to Ditch. It'll save face for Ditch if he's the one ending it. No one has to know it was really you who wanted to end it."

Amberlee laughs to herself. "Sometimes I think maybe you're not naive, you're just full of hope."

"You're my sister, and I love you. I'll do what I can to help you. You've done so much for me over the years. I'll talk to Dom and see what he says."

Her eyes are somber as she nods her head. There's no hope in her eyes. She thinks my conversation with Dom is a waste of time.

"You did great last night. You looked sexy riding Dom. After you both came in here, the party turned into a fuck-fest. Everyone was hot after watching that."

"I was completely consumed. I wasn't aware of anyone around us."

"I noticed," Amberlee smirks. "How'd you like rolling on E?"

"I liked it too much. It's probably something I shouldn't do again, especially if I'm going to feel like this the next day."

"It's worth feeling shitty the next day. That high is incredible. It's my favorite."

"Where do you get the ecstasy from?"

"Dom's probably waiting for you out there. You should get going."

She's clearly evading the subject. I suppose I should accept that the ones who care about me prefer me left in the dark.

"We should do something together. Like dinner and a movie," I suggest. "It'd be nice to have some time with my sister."

Her smile is genuine when it widens over her pretty face. "How about tomorrow?"

"That's perfect."

With my arm through my duffle bag, Amberlee and I enter the living room. My bag drops to the floor and my hand goes to my mouth as I suck in a breath.

"Fuck. Get her in the room, Alee," Dom orders.

Dom is crouched down, helping the blonde woman I saw earlier sip water. She's hardly lucid and around her neck are bold, swollen marks from the belt. Dried blood is below her nostrils.

Amberlee takes hold of my arm, and I shove her off, rushing to the woman.

"What'd he do to her?"

"She was passed out when I found her in the bathroom," Dom tells me.

"She needs to go to the hospital."

Amberlee is standing behind the couch, within my line of sight. She's shaking her head no. "Stay out of it, Erika."

"She needs help," I plead with them.

"I'll take her home. I'll make sure she's ok," Amberlee assures me.

Looking around my empty living room, I realize everyone has left. "He just left her there? Passed out like that?"

The woman reaches to her neck and hisses in a breath. More color is coming into her cheeks. "I want to go home," she rasps.

Amberlee rubs her shoulders. "Dom, will you help me get her to my car?"

One arm under her legs, the other around her back, he scoops up the woman and carries her out of our house. Tears moisten my eyes as the shock continues to overwhelm me.

When Dominic comes back inside, I'm trembling, holding the wall where I left my bag. "I want to leave. I want to leave now."

He tucks me under his arm. "C'mon."

CHAPTER SEVEN

ERIKA

THE RUMBLING of the engine settles and Dominic drops the kickstand. Peeling away from his strong, warm body, I climb off his Harley. Pulling my shopping bag and duffle from his saddlebag, he outstretches his arm for me to take his hand. When I do, he uses it to pull me to him and tucks me under his massive arm.

Together, we walk up his gravel driveway, to his blue siding, two-story house. It's narrow, but tall with a porch across the front. Blue painted pillars hold the roof of the porch up. Being a bachelor's home, there's no decorations or pretty landscaping, but it's well kept with a nicely mowed yard. At the end of the driveway there's a garage and in front of it a silver, two-door, muscle car.

He takes me through the back door which another porch. The back door leads into a fairly spacious and clean kitchen. The tan tile floor is clean and the faux marble counters are free of clutter. An archway leads into a dining room with a black metal and glass dining table and a larger archway into a living room. Stairs ascend to the second floor from the side of the living room. His living room is nice, filled with a black leather sofa, dark wood coffee table, and a large screen TV. His gray carpets are clean and there's no indication of any pets.

Guiding me upstairs, it turns to the right and opens into a hallway. On each side of the hallway are two doors. Taking the open door on the right, Dominic leads us into his bedroom. A large, dark wood bed with a black comforter is center stage. On the farthest wall is a tall, five drawer dresser and to the right of that a closet. In front of the bed is a matching, long, eight drawer dresser with a TV on top of it.

To the left is a door to the bathroom and to the right of that a framed painting or poster of a Harley driving through blazing flames reaching for the sky.

Dominic drops my shopping bag and duffle on the bed.

"Your home is nice. I like it. Better than my...the house I live in."

"I'm not here a lot, and when I am, I'm mostly sleeping. I got a new bed though," he points over his shoulder at it. "It needs broken in." With a wink, he tugs at my shirt, pulling the front of it from my shorts.

My grin is lopsided as I gently move his eager hands away. "I need to brush my teeth and get cleaned up. To be honest, the sight of that woman in my living room still has me a bit shaken." The images of what Drake was doing to her and what she looked like sitting on my couch has put a cork in my libido.

Dominic takes a step back, sheds his jacket, drops it on the bed and pulls his shirt over his head. Nodding toward the bathroom, he picks up my duffle and shopping bag and hands it to me.

"Take care of you. I'll be in shortly."

Leaning up, I give him a kiss that reflects how I feel —grateful. With a slap to my ass, he leaves the bedroom. The stairs creak under his weight as he makes his way downstairs. The bathroom isn't as clean as the rest of the house, but he is a bachelor after all. Everything here is cleaner and nicer than my house though. I already feel comfortable and dread the thought of going home.

With water cupped in my palm, I swallow down the morning after pill, then move onto brushing my teeth. Turning the shower knob to a soothing, warm temp, I climb in. Lathering the soap through my hair relaxes me. As the water pours over my face, rinsing my hair, I hear Dominic enter the shower. Hands on my hips, he pulls me against his front. The length of his cock settles between my legs, teasing my pussy. If I wasn't feeling so dazed by this morning's events, I'd already be wet with need.

Withdrawing my head from the spray of water, I

open my eyes to see his stunning green ones hungry with arousal before his eyes squint, studying my face.

"What's wrong?"

"Every time I close my eyes, I picture her."

Dominic turns me into his arms, holding me close to him in a protective and comforting embrace. Against my neck, he kisses me.

"Let it go," he whispers, his warm breath settling me even more than his comforting embrace has already.

His kiss continues passionately along my neck, raising goosebumps across my skin and scattering the tormenting thoughts in my head. With his hand clasped over mine, he moves it between my legs, plunging my finger into my pussy as his follows. He works my finger and his. My body goes slack, caving to the pleasure. Moans, rushed and bursting, trickle from my lips as the water does from its spout. A powerful hand raises my wrist and pins it against the wall, holding me up as my knees weaken beneath me.

"You ready to take me?"

"Yes."

Grip on my shoulder, he bends me over. Both hands splay out along the wall. He parts my ass cheeks and thrusts into my slick opening. Pounding hard, I'm jolted forward, my tits jiggling as the water streams down my back and the sensation of him filling me washes all thoughts from my mind.

Towel wrapped around me, he fondles beneath the bottom, then chases me to his room as I playfully run from him. I'm seized in his arms and turned, landing on his chest as he lands on his back.

His kiss is deep, loving as he pushes up against the opening of my towel.

"I want you to make an appointment to get on birth control. I'll pay the bill. I want to be able to cum inside you. It's fucking with my head that I can't now. I don't want to keep pulling out and I sure as hell don't want to wear a condom. You feel too damn good for that."

I'm happy to hear him say this. I want the same. Every time he pulls out from me, it leaves me with a cold, yearning sensation like each time he fucks me we're never able to completely lose ourselves to it like we did during the initiation.

"I'll get an appointment as soon as possible. I don't want you to keep pulling out either."

Thumbing my lip, he stares up at me with a raw intensity that wets my core. With his hand to my backside, a single digit toys with my tight hole.

He groans when I let out a quiet pleasured moan.

"Are you sore there?"

"A little," I admit.

Massaging gently, he eases the muscles enough for his finger to slide in. In and out, he pleasures me, his lips taking mine in a demonstrative display of dominance.

"Maybe later, you won't be, that way I can cum in your ass. Did you like me fucking your ass last night?"

Bringing my legs up, I give him better access and

stretch myself more comfortably. Watching me take pleasure in his finger fucking, a wicked grin spreads his lips, brightening his eyes. Taking his hand, I place his finger to my lips, keeping my gaze on his while I suck his finger into my mouth.

"Goddamn, you make me so fucking hard."

Withdrawing his finger, he pulls my towel open. "Ride me, now," he demands.

Finger still in me, I raise up, then lower onto his hardened cock. Laying down on his chest, he squeezes my ass with his free hand, then pushes me forward and back as I rock over him, his finger still pleasuring me from behind, giving me a rush with each thrust.

Sated, clothed, and hair dried, I sit on his couch next to him while we eat the sandwiches I made for a late lunch. With little in his fridge, I still managed to satisfy his hunger, both in the bedroom and in the kitchen.

"We have a couple more things to do. We need to get going," he tells me, popping the last of his sandwich in his mouth.

"What things?"

With a hand on my leg, he rubs along my thigh. "I'm getting you a phone, and I need to have a spare key made for my car, so I can keep the original, and you can have the copy to drive it."

"I have a phone, it's just broken. I haven't been able to get it fixed or replaced yet."

"I'm getting you a phone." My comment doesn't faze

him. "I'm paying for it that way I don't have to worry about not being able to reach you."

I feel awkward about him buying me a phone and getting me a key for his car. I don't want him to think I'm a leech.

"I don't expect you to do things like this for me. Maybe other women have, but I'm not like that."

"Baby, it has nothing to do with what you expect from me. You're my girl and I won't have you being without a car to go places and a phone to reach me. It makes me look like a piece of shit who can't take care of his own woman. Appearances mean something with the Serpents. I'm the VP of the club. You're going to be taken care of. I want you to be taken care of."

Tears moisten my eyes as I pull his face to mine to kiss him. "I can't express how happy I am I met you."

The leather cushions breathe as Dominic stands, taking me with him. Arms around my waist, he rubs my lower back.

"I've been wanting a woman like you." He pulls my chin up, staring down at me, his expression turning serious. "Just don't ever betray me, Erika, and I'll make damn sure your needs are always met."

My lips feather his. With all my heart, I mean every word. "I won't ever betray you."

LEAVING THE STORE, I play with the rose gold phone in

my hand, setting up apps and installing Dominic's number. With an arm around me, I give a sideways glance and he smiles. The kind of smile that shows pride. It's evident how pleased he is with making me happy and caring for me. I'm realizing how important this is to him. I believe it gives him a feeling of being the man I need, and he is, far more than he knows.

"My number in?"

"Yes, thank you again for this."

Stopping in front of his bike, he climbs atop it and tugs me against his side, arm settled at my back.

"You can show me how grateful you are when we get home."

Leaning down, I kiss him, giving him a taste of what I have planned.

When I pull back, his eyes are hooded and glossy. With a squeeze to my ass, he nods for me to climb on.

Slipping my arms around his waist, I hold him tight as he takes off, engine roaring. Wind whipping through my hair, I rest my head on his back and reach between his legs. Rubbing the thick knot in his jeans, I feel him stretch tighter against the material. Placing his hand over mine, he adjusts himself, making it easier for me to feel and stroke along his jeans.

Pulling into the next stop, I'm disappointed how quickly we arrive. I don't want to stop touching him.

Bike parked, he drops the kickstand, and I step off. He yanks me to him, and I climb over the bike, straddling his legs as I face him.

Mouth crashing into mine, he pulls me over his stiff erection. Hair drawn back in his fist, my neck is accessible to his lips and tongue which he ferociously sucks and bites.

"You're teasing me, Sparrow. I can't fuck your pussy right now and it's killing me."

Around us, the gazes of onlookers are drawn to our scene. Neither of us seem to care. I grip his hair in my fingers as his tongue trails across the top of my breast.

"We're heading home after this. I want my cock buried in you."

"Maybe we should have stayed there and fucked all day."

"That's what we're gonna do tonight. No rest for the wicked, baby."

Biting my nipple through my bra and shirt, I squeal, and he smirks, bringing his gaze to mine.

"Let's get in there and get this done, so I can take you home."

Taking my hand, he brings me along inside the hardware store. Fifteen minutes later I have a new key ring and key in my hand.

"It doesn't have the key fob, so I'll give you my key, and I'll keep this one as the spare."

With a kiss, I thank him.

"I'm definitely ready to get back and show you how much I appreciate you."

Within thirty minutes we're outside the main part of town and pulling into his driveway. As soon as he shuts the front door behind him, I slam him against the door and go for his jeans, tearing at them like a wild cat.

His hand fists my hair as my mouth slides up and down his dick.

"Fuck, baby, you really wanted this cock, didn't you?" His head rolls back and I answer with eager sucking and stroking.

Low murmurs and groans slip from his lips when minutes later he comes in my mouth.

Looking down at me, his eyes are full of emotion and contentment. I wipe my lips as he helps raise me to my feet.

"You make me feel damn good." With a brush of his hand, he strokes my face and hair. "Better than any woman ever did."

"Don't talk about any woman you've been with. It makes me want to break something."

Dominic laughs. It's sexy and masculine. "Getting possessive of me?"

"Yes, *very*."

"Good." Hand on my ass, he squeezes tight. "Now you know how I feel."

Standing in Dominic's kitchen, I place the two baked potatoes in the microwave and press start. When I turn, I jump, startled by Dominic's intimidating presence standing in the archway, arms folded, watching me.

"Alee called me to check on you. I gave her your number and told her she could call you herself."

"I bet that surprised her."

"She was happy about it."

Reaching up for two plates out of the cabinet, I feel Dominic's arms wrap around my waist. With a kiss on my neck, his fingers graze along my abdomen making my body tingle from the simple pleasure of his touch.

"I'll get them."

I stay cocooned in his arm as he pulls down two plates.

"The chicken looks good. I'm glad you can cook."

"Been doing the cooking in my house for years. Neither Dori nor Amberlee can cook."

"How'd you end up so different from them?"

"I saw what they did, what happened when they did it, and made better choices instead."

"You're smart. Alee says you enrolled in college."

"I did. I got accepted to the local community college."

The microwave dings and I pull out the two potatoes and gingerly transport them to the empty plates.

Dominic grabs a couple beers from the fridge and takes a seat at the table while I prepare both plates of food. Entering the dining room, I see he's moved one of the vacant chairs close to his. It brings a smile to my lips. I set the food down and Dominic slides one of two beer bottles toward me.

"Looks good."

I raise my beer bottle, and Dominic chuckles,

tapping his against mine. The food is off our plates in less than ten minutes. Dominic sits back, an endearing look of satisfaction on his face.

"That was good."

My reply is interrupted by a few hard knocks at his front door. I start clearing the table as he sees who is on the other side.

"Come in."

Glancing through the archways, I see a tall, light brown-haired man, physically fit, attractive, tattoos all over him like Dominic. He looks through the archways and spots me. I busy myself cleaning the dishes and pan.

"Erika."

The sound of my name draws me to Dominic and the mystery man standing in the living room.

"Erika, this is Christian."

Dark brown eyes study me like I'm the test subject in an examination. I get twitchy under his scrutinizing gaze.

"You're pretty."

I glance at Dominic and he shows no emotion to the statement.

"Thank you."

"It's too bad I missed the show. I heard about it from Roxy."

"She back in your bed?"

"For now."

Christian's daunting gaze returns to me, he licks his

lips before his thumb and forefinger sweep over his scruff.

"You ever had a threesome, honey?"

Dominic's muscles tighten. His body goes rigid. "Don't even fucking think about it."

Christian looks to Dominic and snickers. "Too bad. By the way she's looking at us, I think she'd like it in both holes."

Dominic's hand rubs the back of his neck as he tilts his head and lets out a breath, his nostrils flaring. "Unless you want a knife in your damn gut, keep your dick away from her."

With a quick tilt of his head, Dominic commands me to come to him. Putting me in front of him, he places his arms around me, one hand cupping my breast, kneading it while the other hand dips into my shorts.

My breath catches from the surprise of his fingers rubbing against my clit.

"Tell Christian who your pussy belongs to."

A needy whimper slips from my lips. Dominic rubs harder, making me wet.

Christian's intimidating gaze holds me steady as Dominic continues to work my clit. Raising his chin, his dark eyes are a chilling gleam as he watches me react to Dominic's touch.

"It belongs to you, Dominic. And only you," I say with conviction, glaring back at Christian.

"Good girl," Dominic whispers.

Turning me to face him, his hand draws my lips to his for a provocative kiss.

"Go upstairs and wait for me. Christian and I need to talk."

My ass is squeezed before he releases me.

I go to the steps and begin to ascend, then stop, feeling as though this is something I should hear. Sitting on one of the steps, I eavesdrop on their conversation.

"You got big balls coming into my house and hitting on my girl like that."

"C'mon now, Dom. No disrespect. It wouldn't be the first time we both fucked the same woman."

"Those were sluts. Erika is not a cunt we fuck and toss. She's been initiated and claimed. Pull shit like that again and we'll have a problem."

Christian hums in his throat. "This bitch has your balls in a twist, doesn't she? Her pussy really that good?"

"Did you come for business or just to annoy the fuck out of me?"

"Both. I need you for a job tonight. I know it's your night off, but there's no way around it. I need Carl McGregor roughed up and I know his location tonight only. The son of a bitch moved into our turf and didn't have the respect to get our blessing. He needs a reminder who runs things around here."

There's a moment of silence between them, but I can hear the crinkling of paper.

"Location is on the slip."

"Done," Dominic says with assurance.

"You should bring Erika to the clubhouse. Let everyone have a chance to meet her." Christian's voice is distant as if he's moved toward the door.

"Order a property jacket."

"Sure thing. Let me know when it's finished."

The door closes, and I quickly stand, rushing to reach the top of the stairs. Beneath me, the stairs creak and my heart throbs in my chest as fear seizes me.

"Erika."

Dom's voice freezes my movement.

Slowly, I turn to greet him coming up the steps. His expression isn't difficult to read. He's pissed.

"How much of that conversation did you hear? Don't lie to me either."

"All of it," I reply, my stomach a cluster of nerves.

On the step below me, his form still towers mine. My jaw is gripped in his hand and pulled up.

"You're going to have to learn to respect what I say and obey me."

"I'm sorry." I mean it. My guilt is eating at me as I stare into his angered eyes. I don't want him to ever look at me like this again.

"I believe you." With a swift movement of his arms, I'm whisked over his shoulder. His hand comes down hard on my ass. "But you still need to learn your lesson."

The slap jolts me forward. I hiss in a breath at the painful sting throbbing on my ass cheek.

Tossed onto his bed, his penetrating gaze holds me hostage as he removes his shirt.

"Take your clothes off," he orders.

Eyes a darkened green, I don't see as much of the anger. It's now mixed with lust.

Gaze locked on his, I remove each article of clothing until I'm bare for him, sitting up on my knees.

With a heated gaze, his eyes roam over me, pleased with what he sees. Peeling his gaze from me, he walks to his dresser drawer and from inside he pulls out a pair of metal handcuffs.

"Face down. Ass up. Hands behind your back," he tells me.

You'd think I'd be nervous, trembling from the unknown of what my punishment will bring, but I'm not. The look in his eyes is predatory and it doesn't scare me, it excites me.

Hand to my back, I'm forced forward, my head resting against the soft fabric of his black comforter with my ass at the edge of the bed. Securing both my wrists in his hands, he pulls them behind my back.

The touch of heavy, cold steel clasps around my wrists. Warm hands counter the foreign feel of them by rubbing along my back, massaging my muscles.

Surprise rips through me as the sudden shock of a hard slap comes across my ass cheek.

"I'm disappointed in you."

Another slap and I'm jolted forward. Hands on my hips, he yanks me back. His hardened ridge presses to my ass as he leans forward, cupping my breasts and massaging them in his hands. Nipples hardening, he toys with them between his fingers.

"But you're going to make it up to me," he whispers, feathering my ear.

The bite to my neck sends tingles across my skin. Between my legs, I'm wet and aching for him.

The warmth of his body leaves me, and I instantly miss it, but those thoughts splinter when another slap lands across my ass. Biting my lip, I take another. Fingers probing my pussy, he slides two digits in, and I moan from the mix of pleasure and pain.

"My needy vixen, you want my cock in you, don't you?"

"Yes," my voice is soft, throaty.

"You're not getting it here," Wet with my arousal, his finger withdraws, then presses against my ass. "You're getting it here."

My breath hitches as he slides a finger in. Right away, he adds another, and I hold my breath as he stretches me.

The discomfort soon turns to pleasure with each thrust of his fingers. Rocking against his hand, I moan into the fabric.

When he pulls out, I whimper, and he responds with another slap on my ass cheek.

Behind me, his zipper lowers and his jeans fall, taking briefs with them. The nightstand drawer opens and he takes something out. My attention turns to him and I watch him stroke his cock with the lubricant he's just placed on his hand.

I bite my lip when his cock head presses to my ass. With his size, it causes discomfort and pressure, but that's quickly relieved when he slowly pulls out, then in, his fingers massaging my clit as he goes.

With a hiss, he picks up the pace. "Your ass is greedy for my cock, baby. You take me so fucking good."

One hand cupping my hip, the other takes hold of the cuffs. Arms raised, metal clangs as he fills me deep, pulls out, then slams in, fucking me hard.

Each thrust rips a guttural moan from my lips.

"Oh God, Dom, that feels good."

The cuffs are pulled harder, his thrusts more vigorous. Cuffs dropped, my hair takes its place. My head is stretched back as he pounds into me. When I feel him thicken, my hair is released. Both hands grip my hips. I cry out from the force of his thrusts. It's getting to be too much. I wince from the jumbled blend of pain and pleasure, then he slows, his orgasm filling me.

The slick feel of him pulls out and I'm reacquainted with the stinging sensation of his hand slapping my ass cheek. Face to the fabric, I'm panting short, needy breaths. My pussy lips pulsing with the need for release.

Stepping away from the bed, I hear the dresser drawer open again. Glancing behind me, I can't see what he has. He's hiding it behind him. I moan as he reaches the edge of the bed and slides his fingers into my soaking wet lips.

"Your pussy is aching for me to fuck it, isn't it?"

"Yes," I plead, my voice betraying me, revealing how needy I am.

Lubricant is squeezed out behind me. I expect to feel his head to my opening, but instead, he parts my cheeks and I gasp as something new and unfamiliar is slid into my ass. With a click, it starts to vibrate.

The unfamiliar sensation is incredible. I writhe on the bed, Dominic's fingers caressing my pussy.

"What is that?" I ask keenly.

"A vibrating butt plug. I want you ready for more when I get back."

"Shit, that feels good."

Another click and the vibration ends, leaving me craving more.

"Be a good girl while I'm gone and I'll give your pussy what it wants."

CHAPTER EIGHT

DOMINIC

I NEED to get my head straight. I'm distracted. My thoughts are on my woman in my bed, the new butt plug I put in her ass, and how good it'll feel to fuck her with the vibration turned on. I know she'll love it too. Each time we fuck, I discover how much kink she likes, and damn if I'm not a lucky bastard. She craves it as much as I do.

I know I don't deserve her. She's a pure soul, an innocent falling for the Devil. I'm deceiving her. She believes I'm a good man, but I'm not. I've killed before, and I'll do it again if I have to without care or remorse. But there's something about Erika that makes me believe I'm capable of redemption. Capable of having something good in my life. It's why I can't bring her into my world. It's dark and deadly. She'd be eaten up and spit out, and I'd kill to keep any of my dealings from touching her. Only problem is the Serpents are my life.

How long can I truly keep her locked away, untouched by my sins and my brotherhood?

Sitting atop my bike, I get the signal from my wrecking crew that Carl is inside the Beer Hog's bar. My boots crunch gravel and the cool night breeze whistles as I head inside. Smoke clouds billow near the ceiling, making the already dim lights dull. With a sweep of the bar, I take note of the number of MC jackets, along with non-riders. Only two other riders besides Carl and about fifteen civilians. My plan is simple, in and out quickly and if the other two riders take pursuit, we'll bring them to their knees outside.

The bartender sees us enter. With fear in his eyes, he turns away from the counter and disappears into the back. Smart guy. It's good to have the reputation we do. Makes witnesses less of a problem. Approaching the bar, Carl doesn't notice me at first. Tsk, tsk, his brothers aren't watching his back. They're too drunk and busy getting hard-ons from the chicks in their laps.

The silver metal is warm to my touch. I withdraw it from its case and lean over Carl's shoulder, my left fist gripping his worn leather jacket. With one swift jab, the knife melts through flesh and Carl spits out his liquor, inhaling a sharp breath.

"Be thankful I'm not gutting you. You'll walk away from this, but next time we won't be so lenient. It's our turf. Remember that."

Shoving him forward, I wipe the bloody knife on his jacket. Crimson red is already dripping from beneath.

Knife secured, I land a punch to his jaw. With a thud, his body crashes to the floor.

Attention has been drawn. Time to go. Witnesses turn away at the sight of our colors, but the other two riders are ready for a fight. Tex and Mercy are swinging fists, knocking them down a peg or two. Grabbing their jackets, they shove them outside. One of the women must be an ol' lady since she's beating on Tex's back as he drags her man out the door.

Her last swing is caught in my hand. I squeeze her wrist hard enough to get her attention.

"If you want your ol' man to walk out of here, sit your ass down."

With force, I drive her into the chair behind her. She lands with a resounding thump and extinguishes the fight inside her. A proud sensation fills me as my mouth twists into a wicked smirk. I know Sparrow wouldn't back down if she was in this woman's position and it adds to my respect for her.

The woman's gaze burns a hole in my back as I join the fight outside. Tex has one rider on the ground, fisting his jacket as he lands another punch to his bloodied face. Mercy tosses his opponent to the ground, a kick to his rib cage puts him in a fetal position.

"Let's get the fuck out of here," I order. Looking at the men on the ground, I snicker. "You should've been watching his back."

Tex and Mercy climb onto their rides. Our engines rumble into the darkened night ahead.

ENTERING MY HOME, I clean up in the kitchen, then take the steps quietly, avoiding the stair that creaks. With the lights out, I know she's asleep in my bed. Inside my room, she's tucked under my blanket, only her upper body visible. With the nightstand light illuminating her beautiful skin, I stand there for too long, staring at her, watching her sleep soundly. She's doing something to me. Softening me in a way I didn't think possible.

I even wonder how she'd feel if she knew what I did tonight, that I stabbed another man who didn't get the blessing from the Serpents to start his own club and make deals with our associates. Would she turn away from me in disgust? Would she still look at me with the longing and affection I see each time I touch her? She thinks she needs me to care for her, to protect her, but it's her I need. All of her. Her body, her love, her loyalty.

Beneath my touch, she stirs. "Dominic?"

Gorgeous golden hazel eyes gleam at the sight of me. Raising up, she kisses me, and I move forward, wrapping her in my arm as I roll onto the bed, putting her on top of me. She raises her hips and legs as I move the comforter out of our way.

"Still have it in?"

"Yes," she coos, her expression filled with pleasure as she moves over my growing erection.

"You like it, don't you, baby?"

"I do. It's kept me aroused and waiting for you all night. I want you inside me," she tells me, her tongue lashing at my neck and ear.

Sliding my hands beneath my shirt she's wearing, I remove it. It disappears to my right as I take a good look at her breasts. They're firm, large, and fit perfectly in my hands. Her head tilts back as she pushes her bare pussy against my jeans and I massage her tits. She rides me harder as I squeeze her nipples, pinching them between my fingers.

"Fuck, Dominic, I need you so bad."

Leaning up, I trail my tongue across her chest and bite her neck. Reaching behind her, I press the button. The vibration starts and she releases a moan of pleasured relief.

"It feels so good."

"It's gonna feel even better when I fuck your pussy with it vibrating."

Curiosity and excitement shine in her eyes. Flipping her onto her back, I slide away, undressing quickly.

"Touch your pussy," I tell her.

She does just as I've instructed, and my cock hardens, thick and stiff as I watch her finger between her lips. Her whimpers of pleasure drive me over the edge. A growl slips from my mouth as I climb above her and enter her.

The vibration adds to the stimulation I feel when fucking her tight pussy. With the way this feels, her pussy walls clenching around me as I raise her leg, pounding into her, I know I won't last long.

Her satisfied cries echo in my room as I take her harder.

"Fuck, baby...so damn good."

Everything is lost when I'm inside her. She's my freedom, my drug. My addiction.

Bellowing through her orgasm, her body trembles, and her wet pussy soaks my cock. Gently removing the butt plug from her ass, I take its place, slipping in easily. The incredible sensation draws the blood from my head to my cock. Gliding in and out of her, I thrust deep, several times, fucking her ass good and hard before coming inside of her.

Laying across my chest, her fingers rub affectionately as I caress her body.

"Did you get the butt plug just for me?"

My mouth curves as I chuckle. "Yeah, baby. I've never used it on another woman. I bought it for you."

"Good. I'm sure you've had a lot of women, but I want to be special to you."

Taking her hair and head in my hand, I lean her toward my lips. "You are."

"I was worried about you when you went out tonight."

"Don't be."

Her hazel eyes capture me, something tickles in my chest. Shit, I know this feeling.

"Of course, I'm going to worry. I don't want

anything to happen to you."

"You don't ever need to worry about me. I have my brothers to watch my back and I watch theirs."

Pulling the comforter up, I cover her small frame tucked in my arm.

"The conversation you heard tonight. You can't be listening in on my business. You understand?"

"Yes. I don't like being in the dark though." I can hear the defiance in her tone. "You want me to be with you, but you're keeping that part of your life hidden."

"I have to. The less you know, the more deniability you have. It keeps you safe."

"The Serpents activities are illegal, aren't they?"

She's fishing for information, her thirst for knowledge driving her. I can spare a little to satisfy that thirst.

"Some are. Some aren't."

"The properties?"

"Legal. No more questions."

"One last one. I need to know how involved Alee is. She's my sister. I need to protect her."

"Your sister is street smart. She'll be fine."

Raising on her elbow, her hazel eyes bore into mine.

"Dominic. I need to know."

I adore how she doesn't fear me. She's the only one I know who doesn't.

"Your sister sold your house to Christian as a commitment to the Serpents. She's as much a part of us as a woman can get. We don't allow women to be patch members, but she has earned herself protection as Ditch's property and with her commitment to us. She's now a trusted associate."

"That was the deal? Her loyalty, our house, no one touches me?"

"Yes."

"What does Christian want with the house?"

"That's enough," I warn.

"Fine," her tongue smacks her cheek in irritation. "but what does Alee do for the Serpents?"

"Containment." It's vague. I know it. She won't understand what that means, but it's an answer still. "Is that enough answers or are you going to keep me up for more?"

Scowling, she turns away from me, putting her back to me as she curls up on the other side of the bed. She's angry. It's obvious. Turning to my side, I enfold her in my arms and easily tuck her body against mine. Lips grazing her ear, I reach between her legs and cup her pussy in my hand.

"You can be angry. You can be unsatisfied with my answers, but you don't turn your back on me."

Sliding my finger between her dampening lips, she lets out a tension releasing breath. "I'm sorry. I worry about her."

Laying on her back, she spreads her legs for me. Working her pussy, I attempt to relieve the tension building in her. "I understand the frustration, but your sister does a good job of handling her own shit."

Mouth parting, eyes closed, her body instinctively arches, giving the telltale sign she's giving into the pleasure.

"Damn, baby, how wet you get for me. You're slick with need for my cock already."

Gaze meeting mine, she nibbles her pouty bottom lip. "Alee doesn't want to be with Ditch anymore," she blurts out.

My hand stills. "What?"

Fear fills her eyes. She's concerned she shouldn't have said anything.

"He's abusing her. He treats her terribly. She wants out of the relationship but knows she can't end it. I was hoping you could talk to Ditch."

"Fuck, Erika." Head dropping, I shake it as irritation fills my chest. "You need to stay out of their business."

Anger burns in her gaze as she pulls back from me. Gripping her leg, I tilt my head, shooting her a warning glance.

"He may be your brother, but she's my blood sister. He's hitting her, Dom. In my eyes, he's a piece of shit."

Rubbing my hand over the back of my neck, I step off the bed. I need to think. Cool the fuck down.

"Don't walk away from me," she snaps.

Gaze over my shoulder, my eyes narrow. "Don't push me, Sparrow."

WATCHING her move through my kitchen, cooking us breakfast, a pang of guilt stings me. I was a bit of an ass last night, but I'm not used to caring this much. I'm in a tangled web between wanting to protect her and satisfy her. I may be desensitized to feeling compassion in some ways, but not when it comes to her.

"I'll talk to him. I need to address his cocaine use anyway."

Her body jolts at the sound of my voice. She was lost in thought as she scrambles the eggs.

Attention to me now, an appreciative smile lights up her face. She's beautiful. So fucking beautiful. Her dark, brownish red hair is in some crazy ass messy bun atop her head, her face free of makeup, and she's got my t-shirt over her sexy body, tied at the waist. Her lace panties barely cover her ass and I love being able to see that below my t-shirt.

Setting the spatula aside, she moves into my arms. The warmth of her small frame against my body is a welcomed feeling even if it turns my insides to fucking teddy bear mush. Damn woman.

"Thank you. I'm sorry for being a pain in the ass last night."

"It's ok, baby. It gives me more reasons to cuff you and fuck you."

Her laughter is a melody to my ears. Lifting her chin, I kiss her soft lips.

"You liked everything I did to you, didn't you?"

Pink flushes her cheeks. "Yes, a lot."

"Good. I did too."

Squeezing her ass, I pull her tighter against me, kissing her.

"You ready to eat?"

"I am. What did you make?"

"Bacon and eggs. Your fridge is low on food. I can go shopping for you today," she offers, sprinkling pepper on the eggs.

With a pat on her ass, I give an approving grin. "Do that. Take the car. Get your appointment made too."

Gathering two plates from the cupboard, I hold them out as she fills them with the food. Two cups of orange juice are already waiting on the table. I like this. She knows how to satisfy me in more ways than one. A domestic Goddess. *My* domestic Goddess.

Vibrating on the table, her new phone rings. Has to be Alee. She sits and takes the call.

"Hi... Yeah, this is her... I am... Yes, Thursday at one works great. Thank you."

Excitement spills out of her as she sets down the phone. "I applied for a job. They called Alee and she gave them my number. They want to do an interview."

"No."

Her excitement ebbs. "What?"

"You don't need to be working some shitty job on the side while in college. I want you to focus on getting the degree you want and I want you readily available to me at all times."

Shock morphs her expression. She's processing it, the mental wheels turning.

"What, Sparrow? Spit it out."

"I'm still deciding how I feel about that statement."

"Uh huh...and?"

Twisting the fork in her hand, her brows furrow. "What will I do for my own money? I need a job. I need to pay for books, clothes, food, the bus to take to college."

"Uh huh," I reply casually, biting off a piece of bacon. "So, you're working all the time to pay for those things. When will I see you? When will I have you in my bed? When will you get to study?"

"You'd see me."

"What do you think? Once a week? More, less? I'm not good with that." Just the thought irritates the fuck out of me.

"Dom, I'm not going to live off you."

"You're not living off me. I've told you once, I'll take care of you. I'm not going to keep repeating myself. Call the company. Tell them the interview is canceled."

"I'll think about it."

"You'll think about what?" I reply, dropping the bacon back on the plate. "This isn't a negotiation."

"Yes, it is. I'm grateful for your offer. Honestly, I'm overwhelmed with how incredible you are that you'd even offer it, but I'm not a leech. I'm not going to take advantage of you because you're my boyfriend."

The feet of the chair scrape across the floor as I move it back, rising to my feet.

"I'm not your fucking boyfriend. I'm your man and I take care of what's mine."

STEPPING OUT OF THE SHOWER, she's waiting with a towel in hand. "I didn't mean to disrespect you." Shifting her weight against the wall, her lip slides between her teeth as she watches me run the towel over my cock. "I'm not used to someone caring like you do. I also want you to respect me. To see me as an independent woman who can take care of herself."

Hanging the towel on the hook, I move to where she stands and pull her to me, holding her at her lower back as she looks up at me with adoring propensity.

"The way you're looking at me right now. Whatever you're feeling. That's what I want. I want to be your man, to take care of you, and that doesn't mean I think you can't take care of yourself. I'm asking you for a commitment. If you want to be with me, then you be with me, and knock off the feminism bullshit."

"All right," a smile splits her pretty pink lips, "I'll cancel the interview."

"Good, and now that we're done fighting over that shit, it's time for me to get you wet, and I don't mean in the shower."

CHAPTER NINE

ERIKA

PULLING up to my house in Dominic's silver Camaro, I'm not surprised to see Ditch's bike outside. At this point, I'm pretty sure he's officially moved into the house. With my duffle in tow, I hit the fob, and trudge to the front door. I would've stayed at Dom's, but he left for club business, and after I went grocery shopping, I called Amberlee to apologize for skipping our movie outing. Thankfully, she wasn't upset and was good doing it today.

Approaching the door, I hear tussling inside. Sounds like Ditch and Amberlee are at it again; fucking or fighting. The stench of after party wafts out the door as I open it. Fear, ripe and excruciating seizes my chest when I witness Ditch backhand Amberlee in the face. Without falling over, she takes the hit, her hand instinctively covering the fresh wound. Ditch's deadly gaze fixates on me. His eyes are wild and he's twitching like a damn addict.

Moving between him and her, I straighten my shoulders. "Back the fuck off."

Shoving me, my back hits Amberlee, and she touches my arm. "Don't Erika."

I shake her hand from my arm. "Think you're a tough guy because you like to hit women. You're not. You're fucking garbage. Get the hell out of this house. Now!"

Ditch lunges forward, gripping my hair in his fist. I'm shoved against the couch, his placid cock pushing into my crotch. A harsh ache throbs across my back. Amberlee frantically propels at his side, trying to break him off me.

"Get off her!"

Jaw clenched, Ditch hits Amberlee again. Falling to the floor, tears pool in her eyes. With his attention averted, I claw at his bare arm, then kick outward, catching his leg. It's enough to loosen his grip.

With all my might, I shove forward, crashing us both into the wall behind him. "Get out! Get the fuck out!"

My adrenaline is pumping hard, my heartbeat pounds in my ears. Everything but him is a blur. I'm not stopping until he's gone.

Untamed, his gaze bores into mine. Fearfully, I back up. He lunges again. His hands on my hair and shoulder, forcing me back to the couch. Back arched, I'm propelled backward, my arms flailing as I land on the cushions. Ditch is on me instantly, his grip tightening to the point of ripping out hair.

"You think you can talk to me like that because your Dom's girl?" Pinning me beneath him, he slams his cock against me. "I'm gonna teach you a fucking lesson." Cock hardening, he withdraws from me. My arms swing, making contact with every part of him I can. Forcing my wrists together, he tugs at my jean shorts, unfastening the button. Amberlee is leaning over the couch, clawing at him.

"Get the fuck off her!"

Throat squeezed in his hand, she reaches for her neck as she gasps for breaths. The lethal look in his eyes sends sheer terror coursing through me.

"Let her go! Damn it, let her go!" I scream, bucking and fighting with every ounce of energy I have. Ditch releases her only to backhand her again.

"Stay out of this, Alee or I'll kill you."

Fear has Amberlee frozen, tears run down her red, swollen cheeks as she looks on in horror.

Ditch yanks at my shorts and underwear, pulling them from my hips as I buck and scream.

"Get off me!"

"I'm gonna get off in your fucking pussy. Stop fighting me, you little bitch!"

A slap echoes through the room. My head swings to

the side and everything momentarily suspends in time until the pain vibrates through my nerves, alerting me to the severity of the hit.

Cock pulled from the opening in his jeans, vomit rises to my throat.

The clashing of broken glass forces my senses back to an acute awareness. Amberlee holds the neck of a broken beer bottle as Ditch's heavy body collapses onto me.

"You fucking bastard."

"Alee, help get him off me."

Rushing around the couch, Amberlee and I push and pull until his heavy body lands with a thump on the floor. Touching his neck, I check for a pulse. Thankfully, he has one.

"He's unconscious. I don't know for how long. We need to call Dominic."

Bringing my underwear and shorts back over my hips, I find my fallen phone on the dingy carpet.

Drenched in tears, Amberlee throws her arms around me. "I'm so sorry." She's breaking down before me, emotions and fear running high.

Petting her hair, I soothe her. "Ssh, it's ok. We need to move fast before he wakes up. Can you help me?"

"Yes," she whimpers.

"Find something to tie his hands behind his back. Secure them as tight as you can, Alee. As tight as you can," I emphasize.

Amberlee runs to the garage. Phone in my other hand, I dial Dominic.

"What's wrong?" his tone is concerned. It must be the sound of my voice.

"Ditch is high. He was hitting Alee again. I tried to stop him. He attacked us both. Dom...he tried to rape me."

For a beat, the line is silent. "Where's he now?"

"Unconscious on the floor. Alee hit him in the head with a beer bottle. I'm not taking any chances if he wakes up. I'm tying his ass up."

"Take Alee and go to my house. Don't waste time packing anything. Just go. Don't leave my house until I arrive."

"As soon as he's tied, we're out the door."

I disconnect as Amberlee comes back with zip ties in hand.

"That'll work."

Squatting, I pull his dead weight arms behind him. Amberlee places a zip tie around each wrist and tightens them. I put two more on each wrist, tighten them, then loop three zip ties through the wrists ties to secure his wrists together.

"What do we do now? What'd Dom say?"

Standing, I take her arm, ushering her around the room as I gather my duffle and the key to Dom's Camaro.

"To leave, now. He wants us to go to his house and stay there until he arrives."

Amberlee resists heading toward the door. "I need to grab a few things."

Gripping her arm, I redirect her. "No, you don't. Let's go."

CHAPTER TEN

DOMINIC

MUSCLES STRETCHED TIGHT, my anger is boiling inside me. At my back is Tex, Mercy, and Alcho. The four of us descend on Ditch, dragging him to his feet. With a slap to his face, he comes to, arms still bound behind him.

"Put him on the couch," I order.

Teeth clenched, I lean over him. "How long have you had the cocaine problem?"

"Dominic? What the fuck is going on? Untie me."

"How long?" I bark.

Jumping, Ditch's twitchy eyes focus in on me. With the fear I see in his gaze, I'd say his memories just came back. "Shit...fuck, I didn't touch her."

"How long? I won't ask again."

"A few months. I can quit, Dom. I just need to wean off it."

"Uh huh. You been burning our clients to get your fix too?"

Ditch's lip twitches. His head lolls back as he struggles with the truth and its consequences.

"Not enough for them to notice."

"I see."

Struggling with the zip ties, he squirms beneath my hardened gaze. "C'mon, Dom. Get me out of these things."

Staring into his eyes, I want to kill him. I want to gut him and watch his intestines spill out onto my boots. *No one* touches Erika, but me.

Glancing at the claw marks on his arms, my gaze returns to him and narrows.

"She challenged you, huh? That Erika is a smart-mouthed bitch who needed to learn a lesson. Am I right?"

Lip curling, he snarls. "She got between us. Ran her mouth like she doesn't have a place. It was none of her business."

"Instead of calling me to handle it, you thought you'd rough her up and shove your dick in her?"

"I didn't touch her," he seethes.

Squatting down, I level my gaze with his.

"I think we both know you've been wanting to fuck her pussy for a while now. Only problem was, she didn't want your limp dick, and her sister doesn't want it anymore either, and that fucks with your head, doesn't it?"

"Fuck you."

With a flick of my wrist, I pull the blade from its

sheath beneath my jacket. A sharp, shrill scream fills the house as I cut through flesh and bone, piercing the knife through his leg, just behind the knee.

"You know I don't like being lied to, Ditch. Now tell me the truth." Twisting the blade, saliva dribbles from the corners of his lips as he clenches his teeth through the pain.

"Fuuuuck." His eyes pinch shut as I twist more. "Yes, damn it, I was gonna rape her!"

Leaving the blade in place, I slam my hand into the side of his leg. Grimacing, Ditch's cold brown eyes flicker with fear.

"Here's how this is gonna go. The executive board is gonna meet. We both know the ending result of that meeting is you're gonna be stripped of your colors, but before then, you and I are gonna have some quality time together to work out our personal problem."

With a bob of my head, I gesture for my brothers to step outside.

"Fuck...no. C'mon, Tex, Mercy, don't leave me with him. You're my fucking brothers too."

Mercy turns his body, a merciless stare centered on Ditch. "A brother doesn't cut deals and leave his other brothers at risk of retaliation or a burned reputation, and you sure as hell don't try to rape a brother's ol' lady." With a snicker, Mercy's expression morphs. "You should've known not to fuck with Dom's girl. Now you pay the price."

The door clicks behind them and Ditch's head

slouches. "Do you understand I was high? I wouldn't have tried to rape her if I had my head straight." Pleading eyes raise to mine. "I'm sorry, Dom."

Shaking my head, I rise to my feet. "It's too late for that."

Fist clenching together, I slam it into his face, once, twice, another, until the blood pours over his skin and chest.

CHAPTER ELEVEN

ERIKA

Trembling in my arms, I pat Amberlee's hair, attempting to soothe her as we sit huddled on Dominic's couch.

"He's going to come for me, Erika. He's going to kill me. They'll all rape me and beat me for betraying him, for hitting that bottle over his head."

"No, they won't. Dominic will handle it. He already had plans to deal with Ditch's cocaine use."

"Ditch has lost his fucking mind." With shaking hands, she rummages through her purse, searching for cigarettes. "Dominic is going to flip over him trying to rape you."

Finding her purpose, she pulls the lighter and pack from the bag.

"I'm going out back for a smoke. Can you please find some liquor?"

"Yeah."

Following her into the kitchen, she slips out the back door, and I collect a glass and pour Jack Daniels into it.

The next three hours, I spend waiting on edge, worried about what the fallout will be from today's situation. Finally, shortly after nine pm, Dominic steps through his door. Amberlee is upstairs, passed out in his guest room from drinking a whole bottle of Jack.

Rushing to him, I fill the space between his arms and lay my head on his chest.

"Baby, get me a drink, then join me on the couch."

Returning to the living room, he's removed his colors and I can see the blood spatter on his gray shirt.

Taking the glass, Dominic chugs it down, then pulls me onto his lap. Touching my face, he turns it to examine the bruised skin. Eyes roaming over me, he catches every scratch and bruise.

Reaching between my legs, he settles his hand there, holding me, his thumb gently rubbing me. Looking off, his green eyes turn lethal. "He didn't get his cock inside you, did he?"

"No." Leaning against his chest, I brush my hand through his hair and caress his face, drawing his gaze to me. "Alee stopped him before he could."

Eyes pinched closed, he drops his head back, heaving a sigh.

"I wanted to kill him earlier. Came close to it."

"What happened?"

"We found him tied up where you left him. I questioned him, and he admitted to some things including trying to rape you. I told him he'd be stripped of his colors and then I beat him until he was coughing up blood, gasping for air."

"Good."

Maybe I shouldn't feel that way about his beating, but I do. He's beat my sister enough times, and after what he tried to do to me today, I have no compassion for him.

"What happens now?"

Dominic's forefinger and thumb rub over his stubble. "The board meets, we strip Ditch of his colors, we cover our asses for the shit he pulled. If he comes around, he's liable to get an ass whooping from any of us. If I see him again, I won't hesitate to kill him."

Putting my head to his, I affectionately caress his neck and face. Bringing my lips to his, I pull him from his thoughts, feathering his lips until he gives in to our kiss. Passion sparks between us, our tongues lashing out for the other.

The glass cup clinks on the end table. I'm placed in his hands, then laid beneath him on the couch. Removing his shirt, he caresses my arms as I massage up and down his abs.

"You ok to take me?"

Lust and concern mingle in his eyes.

"Yes. I want you to touch me everywhere. Make me forget his disgusting hands were ever on me."

With a shadow of a smile, he unbuckles his jeans. Undressing us both, he intertwines his fingers with mine as he eases his hardened erection into my slick opening. With each thrust and each kiss, the day's events slip from my mind as I lose myself in the rapturous pleasure he's giving my body.

LYING IN HIS BED TOGETHER, I take another sip of Jack, letting the liquid warm my belly before I curl into his chest. Hand grazing along my side, he kisses my head.

"You know you're doing shit to me, don't you?"

"What do you mean?" I ask, twirling my finger over his chest tattoos.

"I'm feeling things for you a hell of a lot faster than I've ever felt for anyone."

Looking up at him, I admire his intense green eyes. "I don't want that to stop."

"Tell me how you're feeling then."

"I'm completely hooked. I don't want what we have to end."

"You're young though. You might change your mind."

Splaying my palm flat on his chest, I raise myself to view his face and glare at him.

"Don't use the age card. I want you, Dominic. I've wanted you since the first moment I saw you. I'd finger myself fantasizing about you. Call your name when I came. You're better than I expected, and the chemistry is far better than I imagined. I'm all in. Keep treating me like you have, I'll never have a reason to leave."

Dom goes silent, his hand returns to caressing me.

"You're thinking about this because Alee wanted to leave Ditch, aren't you?"

"It got me thinking."

Placing his hand on my face, he brings me in for a heated kiss.

"You fingered yourself thinking about me?"

I chuckle before a smile appears. "Yes."

Eyes admiring mine, I see the emotion in his. It softens them, revealing a side of Dominic I'm certain no person ever gets to see.

"Baby, you shouldn't want me, but I'm a lucky bastard you do."

His fingers caress my neck and get lost in my hair as he rolls us, putting me beneath him, kissing me deep.

Hearing a door open, turns our attention to Amberlee's presence outside of Dom's room.

"I should go check on her. She's scared, Dom, really scared."

Nodding, he places his folded arms on his bent knees as I climb off the bed. "Let her know she's not going to be cast out. She's earned herself enough protection with the deal. I told you...she's street smart."

"What about Ditch?" I ask, pulling a shirt over my head.

"She needs to be careful. Once he's out of the hospital, there's no telling what he'll do."

Walking out of Dom's room, I catch Amberlee in time as she's exiting the hallway door of the bathroom.

"How you doing?"

Crossing her arms over herself, she shivers. "I feel like shit. I'm coming down off E, I've had too much to drink, and I'm worried how this shit with Ditch is going to be handled."

Placing an arm around her, I walk with her back into the spare bedroom. The room is plain and doesn't have much in it, but the bed has a nice wooden head and footboard with a matching nightstand and five drawer dresser.

Sitting with her on the bed, I repeat Dom's message. Relief washes over her fragile features.

"Thank God. I'll ask Dom tomorrow how much interaction I'm allowed with the Serpents, but this is a huge relief. Thank you."

Squeezing me in her arms, she hugs me.

"Have you told Dori what's going on and where you're at?"

"No, I didn't want her to know. She's unreliable. I was afraid she'd let it slip if she's high."

"How'd you get her to agree to the house deal?"

Amberlee's eyes widen.

"Dom told me."

124

"I'm sorry for hiding it from you, but it was my way into the Serpents on my own. It was my own protection."

"I get it, I just wish all the secrecy would stop. I don't like being in the dark."

Rubbing my arm, a smile tugs her lips and then fades. "Dom doesn't want you to know what's going on because he cares about you and so do I."

Looking at her hand rubbing my arm, it warms my chest. "How'd you get Dori to agree? What's in it for her?"

"Cheap rent and drugs."

"Jesus, she's easy.

"She's worse than me," she laughs quietly.

"The drugs, Alee, you need to get a handle on them. You seem high all the time and you've been fired from two jobs already."

Running her hand through her hair, she sighs. "Fuck, I know it. I have a problem. I'll figure out a way to get some help. I don't want to be drugged out all the damn time. It was just hard dealing with Ditch."

Placing my hand on her back, I massage her tired and sore muscles. "I understand that, but you're free from him now, so it's time to get your shit together."

Biting her nail, she pops it free from her teeth. "I will, I promise."

I hope with all my heart she means it. We have our differences, but Amberlee is the only one who has ever cared about me and protected me before meeting Dominic. I owe her so much.

"Should we attempt seeing the movie for the third night in a row?"

"Yes, I need a distraction after work."

CHAPTER TWELVE

ERIKA

Two weeks have gone and I've spent most nights at Dominic's place. A part of me wonders if he'll ask me to move in or even wants me to. Even though I'd say yes without a second thought, I know it's too soon for that kind of commitment. I can't help thinking it though as the last two weeks with him have been incredible.

The rumbling engine of his Harley quiets after he pulls into the parking lot of the Devil's Serpents clubhouse. In front of me is a large, ranch-style building with a second floor over half the building. The siding is painted black and on the porch, next to the front door, is a sign with the Serpents skull and snake emblem emblazoned in silver.

Dominic touches my side, scooping me in his gigantic arm after I climb off his bike. With an arousing graze of his hand, he massages my breast then continues his caress up to my neck and jaw. With his guided hand,

I'm brought to his lips, giving myself to the pleasure of his kiss.

"You sure you're okay being here with me?"

Beneath my fingers his hair is soft from the shower we had earlier.

"Yes, of course. I'm not nervous if that's what you're wondering."

"Good. Tonight's important. Christian has something for you and I want to show you off to my brothers. Not all of them have met you. They're ready to meet the woman who's stolen all my attention lately. After they see you, they'll understand why."

Nibbling my lip, my cheeks flush.

"Maybe I should apologize for keeping you from business."

Grip tightening, he pulls me close, kissing the cleavage of my chest.

"Nah, baby. No need to apologize for satisfying me."

Warmth and wetness linger over my skin from his nibbling lips. Eyes closed, my mouth parts.

"We need to go inside."

"Yeah? You don't want me to bend you over my bike and fuck you here and now? I know you'd like it."

Teasing lips feather across my skin, reaching the outside of my nipple, sending an arousing shiver over my body.

"I do..." My breath hitches when his hand frees my nipple, his mouth ravaging it. Between my legs, my desire burns. "But I don't want your brothers to watch."

A warm breath blows across my damp nipple, taunting my need for him.

"I don't either. I'll take you inside instead."

"Promise?" I ask, gripping my fingers in his hair.

With a hiss, he looks at me with promising green eyes. "Yes."

Walking into the clubhouse isn't much different from being at my house on Serpent party nights. Clouds of cigarette smoke form an artificial ceiling above, dimming the ugly yellow lamps. Bold, skull and serpent emblems are like a sea of snakes before me. They're everywhere I look. Beer bottles and liquor glasses clang on the tables in unison with the loud boisterous voices and music. I'm surprised to see a few jackets and vests that display MC club emblems other than the Serpents. I look to Dominic.

"You allow other club members in here?'

With me in tow, he guides me to a table of Serpents I recognize.

"Just the bar and restaurant part of the clubhouse." He points toward double doors on the left wall of the darkened room. "Not past those doors. That's our personal clubhouse."

A Serpent I've come to know as Mercy removes his arm off an empty chair. Dominic sits in it, pulling me into his lap.

A young prospect, not much older than me tilts his beer. "What can I get you to drink, Dom?"

Pride flashes in Dominic's eyes when he brings his attention to the prospect.

"Two beers, two shots of whiskey."

"You got it."

With ease, he slips from his chair, headed toward the bar on the backside of the room. Dominic's thumb slides into my jeans. Caressing me, he quickly falls into conversation with his brothers about their last ride and some club drama.

"Drake and Levi were bitching about how you handled Ditch's actions," Mercy shares.

His caressing stops. Fingers tightened, I know he's holding back his real emotions, shielding them with an expressionless face.

"Yeah? Tell me about it."

Tex's eyes roll over my chest and face, then settle on Dominic with a seemingly careless expression. "You know how that clique of whiny asses are. They're a bunch of boys trying to look out for one another."

"If they got something to say, they should bring it to the board or to my face."

"They haven't been around much since Ditch got out of the hospital," Mercy tells him behind a beer bottle headed to his lips.

This time, my muscles tighten and Dominic's hand lifts to my back, caressing me as several eyes around the table take notice of my reaction.

"Excuse me," I mumble, rising from his lap.

Standing, Dominic takes my hand, stopping me.

"Where you goin', Sparrow?"

"Bathroom and to check on Alee."

"What's she doing tonight?"

"I don't know which is why I want to find out."

The prospect returns at a perfect time. Gathering one of the shots out of his hand, I down it, set it on the table and veer off toward the bathroom.

Exiting the stall, I pull my cell from my jeans pocket. The call to Alee is ringing by the time I step out the bathroom door. A hand touches my shoulder and my attention averts to the owner.

"Erika, right?"

My thumb taps the *End Call* as I stare up at Christian's unreadable brown eyes. Wearing his colors, he stands tall, nearly as tall as Dominic. His presence is dominating, and my body responds, jittery and apprehensive.

"Yeah."

"Come to my office. I have something for you."

Nerves bunch in my gut. I want Dominic with me, but I'm afraid to disrespect him.

"Ok."

Following Christian's back, I'm led through the hall, right, down a second hallway, then right again into his office. There's no one back here and my jittery nerves have my body tingling. Closing the door behind me, my back hits wood as Christian turns on me, caging me between him and it. Fear courses through my veins as my brain struggles with how to respond.

"Did he really try to rape you or are you a lying cunt?"

Arms braced next to my head, I have nowhere to go. Swallowing the lump in my throat, I gather my courage.

"He did. He was high on coke and wouldn't stop beating on me and Alee. He was about to rape me when Alee hit him over the head with the bottle. I swear, Christian, I would never lie to Dom."

A piercing gaze narrows, studying my face. Never wavering from his stare, I await his response.

"Make the mistake of betraying us and I'll hurt you, Erika. I'll make you bleed."

I release the breath I was holding when he lowers his arms.

"Is this how you treat all the women the Serpents date?"

With a click of his tongue, a glimpse of a smirk appears and disappears just as quickly. "Dom said you have a smart mouth. Learn to keep it under control around me. I'm not Dom. I don't have a soft spot for you."

"I'm not trying to disrespect you. You clearly don't trust me, maybe don't like me. You don't have any reason to feel either way."

"Telling me how I should feel about you isn't helping your stance. I see you as a short-term fixation for Dom. A convenient distraction."

"I'm not a fuck and dump for him if that's what

you're implying." Heat rises to my cheeks. "I didn't expect you to be such an asshole."

That same smirk reappears. "You have just as much guts as you do ignorance. You're new to the Serpents, so I'll let it slide. This one time."

"It has nothing to do with guts or ignorance. It has to do with the fact that I want your respect and I won't put up with the way you're treating me now."

Hand gripping my face, I'm shoved against the door.

"If Dom hadn't claimed you as his, I'd shove my cock into your smart mouth until you learned how to shut the fuck up."

Glaring at him, I yank my jaw from his hand. Beneath my fear, my anger surges.

"Did you actually have something to give me or did you just want a chance to put me in my place?"

With a snicker, he turns toward his desk. For the first time, I take in his office. It's small, but not crowded. A brown desk is off to the right with a chair sitting in front of it. To the left is a trophy case with a few motorcycle memorabilia inside. Next to that is a wardrobe closet. Reaching inside, he pulls out a black jacket. Tossing it to me, I catch it in my arms. Spreading it out, I see it has three patches; Serpents, Property of, and Dom.

"It's an honor to receive one of those. Try to respect it."

Placing my arms through the sleeves, I put it on.

Right away it feels like a security blanket, an extension of Dom's protection.

"I'd be a fool not to."

Hardwood hits my back and I step forward as Dominic enters the office. Relief spreads through me. With one look at me in the new jacket, his eyes glisten with satisfaction.

"Looks good on you. Turn around."

I do, and he reads the back, then steps forward, encasing me in his giant protective arms. "Fits perfect." With a kiss on my neck, I catch the scent of whiskey. "I think it's time to give you a tour of the place."

Behind me, I sense his attention switching to Christian.

"Thanks for gettin' this taken care of."

"Never thought I'd see you get one."

"Things change," Dominic responds casually.

Like a moving shadow, a strange expression crosses Christian's face. "So I've noticed."

Dominic laughs, a deep guttural laugh. I feel like the outsider of an inside joke.

"You should teach her what respect means around here, Dom. It'd be good for her to learn it. She's worse than an ignorant hang around."

"Erika, step outside."

With Dominic's insistence, I'm ushered toward the door. Stepping out, I take a breath of relief I'm no longer in Christian's presence. Curiosity piqued, I stand by the door and listen.

"Don't ever tell me how to handle my woman. She's not used to how we do things, but she'll learn. Now tell me what the hell has you so pissed off."

Heavy boots thud the floor.

"We lost a brother and some members are angry about it. It's causing a rift in the club. All over some pussy. How well do you really know this girl? You know how much of a slut Alee is. I fucked every hole that bitch has before Ditch claimed her. What makes you trust her sister?"

"I don't give a shit what her sister chooses to do. She's not her. We both know you can't compare them. We both lost family members that were weak. We're nothing like them."

"I'll trust your judgment, but I don't want this chick getting in the way of our brotherhood. You know what I'm saying? She's caused enough trouble with this shit with Ditch."

"Ditch deserved what he got. He crossed the line when he tried to rape her, and it wasn't just the rape. He was burning clients to get his fix. He was putting the entire club at risk of retaliation because of his dumbass choices. Ditch is weak and you know it. We don't need a brother like him in the Serpents. If his closest brothers want to try to impeach me, let them. I'm not worried about a few votes from some childish, pissed off brothers. And don't go getting your fucking panties in a twist because it's the first time you've seen me give a damn about a woman."

"Not the first, Dom. The first time I've seen you care this much, this quick."

"Is what it is. Don't question it. Got my back, I got yours."

"Always, brother."

The doorknob jiggles when a hand lands on it.

"We done here?"

"Yeah, enjoy your night with your girl."

Rushing down the hall, I put my cell to my ear to call Alee.

"Erika."

Hitting end, I turn to face Dominic.

"Were you listening the whole time?" With a curve of his mouth, his expression is playful, not angry as I somewhat expected.

"Yes," I admit, blushing.

"I knew you were. Can't help yourself, can you?" he asks, pulling me into his arms, resting his hands on my back.

"No, Christian was an asshole to me when we were alone. I wanted to know what he said after I was gone."

Dominic's brows furrow. "Let's take a tour and we'll talk."

Down the hall, and through the main bar to the brown, wooden double doors, we enter a comfortably sized conference room. It's clearly used for meetings. In the center, the wooden table has the Serpents emblem carved into it. The beautiful craftsmanship is detailed, and with lacquer, the wood shines.

"This is our church where we have our meetings."

Leaning against the table, he pulls me to him, settling me between his legs. Outside the room, music booms, but the solid wooden doors create a buffer.

"Tell me what happened before I showed up to his office."

Apprehensive, my eyes wander around the room, taking in the signs, posters, and the self-serve bar cooler in the corner.

"Sparrow, look at me."

Pulling my face to his, he captures my gaze with his intent one.

"Christian and I go way back, he's fiercely protective of the Serpents, but I still want to know every detail of what was said and done. Don't be nervous to tell me."

With a breath, I resign myself to sharing it all.

"As soon as we entered the office, he turned on me, pinned me to the door and demanded to know if I lied about Ditch trying to rape me."

Dominic's thumb grazes my back. "Keep going."

I share the rest and Dominic's expression goes from hardened to a softer empathetic expression as he swipes a thumb affectionately across my cheek.

"I know what he did pissed you off. I want you to understand that was his way of looking out for me. It's his job as the President to look out for every member and he and I are especially close. To him, you're an outsider, but that will change in time. Until then, avoid being caught alone with him. As for putting his hands on you, I'll deal with that."

Still worried about Alee and not in the mood to party, I lean my head against his chest.

"Thank you for the jacket and for giving a damn about how that conversation made me feel."

With a hand through my hair, he pulls my head back so I'm looking up at him.

"Learn to expect that from me. With that jacket, you're an extension of me. If my brothers disrespect you, they're disrespecting me. I don't like you being alone with any man, not even Christian. I know he snuck time alone with you, so he could test you. But I don't like it. Don't ever let him do that to you again. You're mine, Sparrow. You belong to me and no one else. That means no one has the right to touch or chastise you. Only me and only the way I want to."

With the way his dominating gaze stares down at me, heat warms between my legs.

"When you say it like that, that I belong to you, it turns me on. I want to be yours. With you I feel safe, free, wanted."

Hand over the knot in his jeans, his gaze turns lascivious.

"You know a brother could walk in here and see me taking you?"

"I don't care. I want you."

"Good, baby, because I'm bending you over this table and pounding your pussy."

Mouths craving the other, our tongues lash back and forth. Hands on my jeans, he unfastens them and slips a hand inside my underwear. At the touch of his skilled fingers, my hands race to unbutton and unzip his jeans.

"I need you. Always need you," I breathe against his mouth.

"I know you do, baby. I love that about you."

Pulling his cock free, he ravages my mouth as I stroke him up and down.

Gripped in his hands, I'm whisked into the air, my back hitting the table.

"Don't be shy about expressing how you feel." Removing my jeans down my thighs, he winks before lowering between my legs.

Tongue to my clit, he sucks and nibbles before slipping his tongue between my pussy lips. Writhing against his face, I unleash pleasured moans, not giving a fuck who hears me.

"Oh God, Dominic, more."

With a finger slipped inside me, he moves it in and out, getting it wet, then pulls it out, placing it at my ass. Filling my backside, he pumps in and out, as his tongue works my pussy. Cries of unrestrainable pleasure burst from my lips. My orgasm frees my body and he backs away as I quiver from the aftershocks.

"There's nothing more beautiful than you coming apart for me." His hands caress the inside of my thighs. "Now turn over, baby. I'm not done with you yet."

With my legs in his hands, he flips me, pulls me to

the edge and spreads my cheeks for a better view. Sliding into my soaking wet opening, he holds my hips tight as he pounds into me, taking my pleasure to another level.

Hair winding in his hand, the other left on my hip, masculine growls escape his body as he pounds harder, thrusting his cock deep inside me.

Pulling out, another orgasm ripples over my body as hot cum lands across my lower back and ass.

With a slap to my ass, he leans over the side of me, pulling my head back for a passionate kiss.

"This jacket, you bent over the Serpents table, my cum all over your ass, I'm on cloud nine."

I kiss him back, feeling everything he's feeling. With a grin, he easily rips my panties from my legs. I laugh from the shock and surprise of it.

"Dom!"

Wiping off his cum with the fabric, he smirks. "You're sexier without them anyway."

Raising his briefs and jeans over his hips, he fastens them and walks to the nearby trash can and tosses the ruined underwear in it.

My own jeans are back in place when he returns to me. Sitting against the table, he maneuvers his hands to my thighs, raising my legs around his waist.

Head to mine, he looks me in the eyes. "Promise me you won't ever ruin what we have. I don't think I'm capable of letting you go."

"I don't want you to ever let me go. It would ruin me."

Eyes closed, Dominic appears deep in thought, still holding me close to him.

"Fuck, you make me crazy. Let's get out of here before I say any more pussy whipped shit."

With a quick kiss, he drops my legs and slaps my ass as I turn toward the double doors. Phone ringing, I stop and pull it from my back pocket.

"Alee, what's up?"

"I'm sure you're busy with Dom, but I don't know...I thought...maybe...you could come home tonight instead of staying at his house."

The tension in her tone has me on alert. "What's wrong?"

"Dori has a new boyfriend who's a fucking perve, and Ditch has been calling me, leaving me threatening voicemails all day. I'd feel better if you were around, you know? Just for tonight."

Looking at Dom, I know he sees the pleading expression in my eyes.

"Yeah, I'll come home."

With a tap of the button, I end the call and place the phone back in my pocket. He's already studying every detail of my face and body language.

"What's up with Alee?"

"Will you be upset if I ask you to take me home? I'm worried about Alee. She's scared. She asked if I'd come home tonight and hang out with her. Ditch has been calling her all day leaving her harassing voicemails."

With a hand to the back of his neck, his eyes roll. Head falling back, his gaze goes to the ceiling. "Fucking Ditch."

Attention back on me, he grazes my face. "Yeah, I'll take you home. I'll stay the night with you there."

Wrapping my arms around him, I hug him. "Thank you."

His hand settles on my waist as he looks at me. "You wantin' to head over there now?"

"If that's all right with you, yeah."

"It is. Let me tell my brothers, then we'll head out."

CHAPTER THIRTEEN

ERIKA

ENGINE QUIETING as we stop in the driveway of my home, I notice the new motorcycle that must be Dori's new boyfriend's. I wonder what kind of winner she's picked up this time. Thankfully, being at Dominic's house nearly every night, I've been able to miss out on meeting him.

Taking my hand, Dominic leads us inside the house. Sure enough, it reeks of its usual scents of sex and drugs. What's worse is we get a dimly lit show of Dori and her new beau fucking in the kitchen. Seeing us, they come to an abrupt stop, and I grimace at the disgusting sight. Folding her dress down, he turns his back to us as he puts himself away.

With a grumble, Dominic's hand tightens, pulling me into my room. Behind us, he closes the door, then stands guard by it, arms crossed, muscles tight.

"Alee conveniently left out a detail about your

mother's new fuck buddy. He's a rival gang member. Pack your shit, Erika. You're not staying in this house anymore. It's filthy enough as it is, and now, your mom's brought trash into it."

Startled, I stand there processing what he's said.

"Now, Erika," he barks. "Only the necessities. I'll get you whatever else you need."

"What about Alee?"

"Fucking Christ." He shakes his head. "I'm seconds from opening this door and stabbing the fucker in the other room. Hurry up and pack. She can stay at my house tonight."

"Don't do that," I reply in a panic. Rushing around my room, I gather what I absolutely need and stuff it in my duffle bag.

A knock on my door tenses my whole body. Dominic's jaw locks, his muscles bulging as he opens the door. On the other side stands the rival MC member. Long, greasy hair lies on both sides of his shoulders with a matching lengthy beard making a V shape down his chest. He's a big guy like Dominic, but his eyes don't hold the same kind of lethal stare that Dominic's does.

"How much to let me have a jab at her pussy?" he leers, words a drunken slur.

Fists clenching, Dominic gives no warning. He crashes through the threshold of my door, fists gripping the man's vest as he slams him into the wall. The sound of cracked wood and plaster indicate the force Dominic used. Watching fists fly through the air, I'm left in a daze of fear and shock as both men lunge at one another, intent to injure the other.

Dori and Amberlee's screams breach the other side of the men. There's no way for me to get out and no way for them to get to me.

Frozen in fear, I can't look away as blood spatters the walls and angry grunts bellow out from their chests. I know Dominic won't stop until this man backs down or is dead. I'm terrified of the latter outcome.

Screaming at them, Dori threatens to call the police. A tinge of worry hits my chest she might make things worse.

"Dori, no. Stay out of it!" I scream. "It's your fault you brought this asshole into our home!"

Hearing a frightening crack of bone, I jump in place, seeing the rival MC member slump to the floor. Blood is pouring from his nose and his jaw appears dislocated. Dominic surges forward toward Dori. Amberlee moves out of his way, and Dori backs up, clearly afraid.

"You don't ever bring a rival club member into this house, you dumb whore! If I hadn't been here, he would've walked into her room and fucked her without a care. It's bullshit how little you care for her. Say your goodbye. She's moving in with me. I won't have her living with an unloyal, cracked out whore like you."

Turning on Amberlee, she cowers beneath his rage.

"You knew this fucker was here. You should've

warned me. This just might cost you your in with the Serpents."

Guilt and discomfort slam into my gut hearing the way he's talking to my mother and sister, but so much of what he said is true.

Fuming, his gaze switches to me. "Erika, we're leaving, now."

With a couple steps forward, he outstretches his hand for me to take it so he can help me climb over the slumped and bloodied body blocking me in. Seeing his face and skin already bruising and covered in crimson red tears a hole through my gut.

Taking his hand, I tug the duffle along with me and jump over the guy's body. Dominic catches me at the end of my leap and settles me on my feet. With my hand in his, he leads us toward the door.

"You're going to let him talk to me like that, then leave with him?" Dori's voice screeches, her expression appalled.

Stopping in my tracks, I glare back at her. "Yeah, I am. Dominic actually gives a damn about me. I can't say the same for you. What you did tonight was stupid. You had to have known they were rivals, but I'm guessing the money or drugs were more important."

Seeing my jacket, her eyes narrow. "So you're one of them now? His little whore for the taking?"

Dominic steps forward, ready to defend me or hit Dori, I'm not sure which. Placing my hand on his arm, he stops, looking over at me.

"Yeah, mom. That's all I am. Just a whore for the taking. I don't expect you to see me as anything more."

Alee comes in close, tears in her eyes. "I'm so sorry. I didn't realize this would all go down like this."

Pulling my wallet from my bag, I retrieve a hundred-dollar bill from it and hand it to her.

"Dominic was going to let you stay at his house tonight, but I know that's not happening now."

She glances at Dominic, regret filling her irises. Looking back at me, she takes the bill.

"Stay at a hotel tonight. Call me when you've checked in. I want to know you're safe." Hugging her, tears well in my eyes. "I know you didn't mean for this to happen," I whisper.

Dominic wraps an arm around me. "Let's get out of here."

CHAPTER FOURTEEN

DOMINIC

IN THE SHOWER, I can hear her crying. I want to go to her, to hold her until her tears stop, but I know she needs this time to cry out her emotions and to find the strength that comes after. She chose me tonight, without hesitation, but I know the fight we had with her mother hurt her. Deep down, no matter how much her mother has done to her, she still loves her and loves Amberlee even more. Giving Amberlee that money for a hotel was smart. I'm proud of how she handled the entire situation.

Seeing the way she didn't second guess coming with me proved to me where her loyalty lies. From the moment I kissed her in that shitty kitchen and tasted what she had to offer me, I knew I wanted her, all of her, and most importantly, her devotion to me. In the short time we've been together, I can see that devotion growing, see how strong her feelings are for me. There are moments I worry I'm letting this happen too fast, but I've never been the kind of guy who lives life cautiously. I'm a live free, live fast, live hard kind of guy. Yet I know it's true, she's becoming my Achilles heel. My one and only weakness. I find myself willing to put her before my brothers and *that* is dangerous.

Brotherhood and respect are the reigning principles of the Serpents. Without them, we wouldn't be as strong as we are, which is why stripping Ditch of his colors was an easy choice for me and many others. Why Christian is indulging Drake, Levi, and probably Shane's complaints is complete bullshit. He needs to set them straight and be done. Maybe he was closer to Ditch than I realized. It would give another explanation to him cornering Erika and questioning her about the attempted rape besides only looking out for me and the Serpents.

Jesus, I need to stop. She has my head so fucked I'm questioning Christian's intentions. Laying back on my bed, arm behind my head, I stare at the ceiling.

1. Need. To. Get. My. Shit. Together.

My brothers rely on how logical, controlled, and focused I am. Tonight, I wasn't controlled. Seeing the way that fuck, Bronx, looked at Erika, what he wanted to do to her, it lit my mind on fire. I saw red. He's lucky he was knocked out unconscious. I would've killed him. I would've killed Ditch for touching her too. Fuck, I'll take out any man who thinks they can lay a hand on her. These pansies don't know what I'm capable of. What I'll do. All because they've never seen me with a woman like this.

I'm getting tired of having to make it clear who she belongs to. I didn't want to do it to her, but I might have to bring her back to the club to claim her again in front of every Serpent and any other club member who's around.

Just the thought of fucking her on one of the pool tables while everyone watches is giving me a hard-on. I'd get a high from her moans and the sound of her voice when she cries out my name for everyone to hear. Only one problem. She brings out a possessive side of me that puts me in a rage anytime a man looks at her like he wants to fuck her. There'd be many looks like that and that's just asking for a mass murder.

Hearing the bathroom door open, my thoughts disperse like frightened rats. Padding across the room, a towel wrapped around her, her damp hair in thick strings around her face and shoulders. Sad, swollen, puffy eyes tug at my blackened heart. I open my arm for her, and she crawls into it, laying against my body.

Tilting my head to the nightstand, I bring her attention to the glass sitting there.

"I brought you some whiskey. Thought you might need some after the shit that happened tonight."

"I'm so sorry Dori did something that stupid." In her tone, I can hear tears threatening to escape again.

"Baby, look at me."

Lifting her chin, her glistening golden hazel eyes plead with me for forgiveness.

"You don't need to be sorry. You can't help the decisions Dori and Alee make. I won't ever hold the things they do against you. I want to be sorry for the things I said to your mother and sister because I know it hurt you, but they needed to hear them."

Nodding, she fights back tears. Pulling her on top of me, she spreads her legs over my semi and leans her chest against mine. Removing the fabric of the towel from between us, I enjoy the feel of her naked skin warm against mine.

Hands on her ass, I pull her pussy tight to my growing erection. "You're hurting still. I want to fix it. I'll do anything you want. Tell me what you need."

"Will you make love to me? Like you did the night Ditch hurt me?"

"Yeah, baby, I can make love to you." Taking the glass from the stand, I hand it to her for her to drink. She takes it, gulps it down quickly and grimaces at the bite.

Turning her on her back, I trace my fingers with slow, languid motions up her thigh, waist, and across her breasts, twirling my fingertip around her nipple before plucking it between my thumb and forefinger.

My eyes catch hers, the light of the lamp and the fire of the whiskey dancing in her gaze.

"Do you love me, Sparrow?"

Lips trailing across her left breast, her body arches in response.

"I'm completely in love with you."

A single tear falls from the side of her eye.

Leaving a trail of damp kisses, I bring my mouth between her legs.

"What does love mean to you?"

With a kiss on her thigh, I tenderly spread her legs.

"There's nothing I won't do for you. You're everything to me."

Kissing between her legs, her body quivers, needy for my touch.

"Every man has a weakness. I didn't have one...until I met you."

CHAPTER FIFTEEN

ERIKA

WAKING up in our sex-scented and well-used sheets, I'm disappointed to see Dominic is gone. Rolling over, I lift my cell phone from the nightstand and read the text message he left me.

Didn't want to leave your sexy ass this morning but had to take care of business. Be home late.

Bummed I won't see him until tonight, I pad to the bathroom and draw a bath. After breakfast, I empty my duffle and toss it over my shoulder with the intention of refilling it with more of my things from home, my old home. That's going to take some getting used to.

Worry grinds in the back of my skull. I can only imagine what it was like for Amberlee and Dori when Bronx woke up from his fight with Dominic. If he's still there, I won't be going in, but maybe Amberlee can get away and spend some time with me since it's the weekend.

Locking the back door, I traipse to the Camaro. My footsteps slow when I see two officers stepping out of a police vehicle in Dominic's driveway. They spy me and I freeze.

"Miss Daniels."

Shit. I know this routine. Been down this road before with my father.

They approach, kind smiles, pristine uniforms. I have nothing against them but seeing them is never a good thing.

"Miss Daniels, is Mr. Xavier home?" The taller one with a handsome bearded face asks.

"No, he's not."

"Do you know where he is?" With darker features and a hardened expression, his partner comes off less congenial and more all-business.

"I honestly don't know. He was gone before I woke up and he left me a message that I'd see him later."

Vague is best. Never too many details.

"That's fine, ma'am. We'd actually like to speak with you today. Would you mind answering some questions for us?"

"Am I being arrested or detained?"

"No ma'am," the taller officer responds.

"Go ahead then."

Leaning against the Camaro, I watch them take out their notebooks and pens. Next, I'm given my rights and right to refuse to answer any questions. All things I've heard before.

"Do you know what you were doing on the night of July thirteenth?"

"That was over a couple weeks ago."

I was here with Dominic. It was the night...oh my God, it was the night he went out for Christian. The conversation I eavesdropped on.

"Yes, ma'am, it was. Do you remember what you did that evening?"

"I was here."

"Do you remember where Mr. Xavier was that night?"

"Yes, here with me."

"Did he leave that evening for any reason?"

Keeping my attention on them, I stand confident. "No, he was with me all night. We had sex a lot that night, so I remember it well."

Cheeks blushing, the taller one scribbles in his notepad.

"Did anyone come to visit that night?" the shorter officer asks, brown eyes studying me closely.

Behind us, the engines of Harleys rumble down the road. Attention shifting, the officers briskly walk to their vehicle, and I follow. Four Harleys and their Serpent riders block the officers' vehicle from exiting. Expression cold and deadly, Christian steps off his bike.

"Erika, get on."

Glancing at me quickly, his expression brooks no argument. Moving with sure steps, I head to his bike. His gaze remains fixed on the officers.

"We're not done here," the shorter officer tells Christian.

"Unless you're taking her in on a charge, you're done."

Climbing onto Christian's bike, I watch the officers back down from the challenge. Christian climbs on his ride and leads the crew off down the road. This feels bad, real bad, especially with Dominic missing.

Pulling into the clubhouse, Christian cuts the engine and I hop off quickly. Snagging my wrist, he gets my attention.

"What'd you tell 'em?"

"Not a damn thing. It's not my first rodeo with the police, Christian. I assume you know who my father is."

Christian clicks his tongue as he nods. "Yeah, I know. So what'd they ask you?"

"Where I was on July thirteenth and where Dominic was. I told them he was with me, fucking me all night."

A smirk lifts the corner of his mouth. "Good girl. What else?"

"They asked if anyone came to visit that night?"

"And," Christian's gaze narrows.

"And you arrived, saving me from having to lie and tell them no one came to visit."

Christian gives a nod of approval as he climbs off his bike.

"You did good."

Looking around for Dominic's bike, I don't see it.

"Where's Dominic?"

"He's being detained at the station. They took him in this morning. Don't worry though, he'll be out by tonight."

He must have read my expression.

"What do they have on him?" I ask, panicked.

"A couple witnesses, but we'll take care of them."

Following Christian's back, I'm surrounded by Serpents as we enter the clubhouse.

"What are you going to do to them?"

The tall, ginger-haired man next to me snickers and I recognize him right away. "Mercy, right?"

"Yeah and don't worry your pretty little head. Us Serpents take care of our own. You can hang with us today until Dominic is out. He asked us to pick you up as soon as he got rolled on."

"He knew they'd come to his house looking for me?"

The men disperse in the clubhouse, leaving me alone with Mercy.

"Yeah, the police are predictable. You're a fresh target. They don't know how loyal you are to Dominic yet. They were hoping you could help them incriminate him."

"There's no way in hell I'd let that happen."

Mercy's thumb and forefinger swipe over his scruff as he licks his lips. "That's what Dominic said too." With a tilt of his head, he motions toward me. "Where's your jacket?"

"In my bag."

"Put it on while you're here. I don't want any of

these dumb fucks getting the wrong idea about you being here. One Daniels sister is enough."

Pulling my jacket from the duffle, I look at him confused. "What do you mean one Daniels sister is enough?"

Mercy blows out a puff of air. "Your sister showed up here last night wanting to work herself back into our good graces."

"And?"

"You're a sweet thing, aren't you?" he chuckles, clearly humored by something. "Your sister whored herself out."

Vomit rises in my throat and I slap my hand over my mouth. Mercy puts a hand on my shoulder, stabilizing me.

"Ah, fuck, you look like you're gonna be sick. Phil, bring me a bottle of water," he shouts at another Serpent.

"She still here?"

"Yeah, she's somewhere around here, probably with Christian. He took her up on her offer to satisfy him."

"Stop fucking talking."

Mercy laughs, his hand gripping my shoulder, keeping me from lunging forward and spilling my breakfast.

Phil joins us, handing the water bottle to Mercy. He slaps it into my open palm.

"There she is now."

Walking out from the hallway that leads to

Christian's office, is Amberlee and Christian, his arm is draped around her shoulder. Purple marks of exhaustion are under her eyes, yet she seems full of energy, spritely even.

Christian slaps her ass in the little shorts she's wearing and her braless chest bounces in her flimsy camisole. "That was fun last night, Red. We'll have to do it again. Now be sure to give my boys some attention too."

Phil eyes Amberlee's ass and makes his way toward her as she watches Christian walk back down the hall.

"Hell no." Intent on ending this shit show, I storm toward Phil and Amberlee. Mercy grips my jacket and yanks me back to him, whispering in my ear.

"Listen, sweet thing. Not every Serpent has a pretty woman like you to satisfy them, so that's where your sister comes in. She's keeping the men happy and she gets what she wants in return. Don't get in the way. I told Dominic I'd keep an eye on you, and that's what I intend to do, so don't start a fight I have to end."

Brushing him off my sleeve, I glare at him. "I'm guessing Dominic told you I'm a smart mouth who doesn't listen to anyone and if he didn't, he should of."

I'm out of his reach before he can grab me again.

"Amberlee!"

Whipping around at the sound of my voice, her expression is horrified.

"What the fuck are you doing?"

"Goddammit, Erika, what are you doing here?"

159

Phil, a shorter guy with a round belly wraps an arm around Amberlee's waist.

"This your sister?"

"Yeah," Amberlee replies, unfazed by his groping.

Mercy is at my back, breathing down on me like a freaking lion that's just caught its kill. I need to tread lightly. I know I'm in over my head.

I look to Phil and put on the charm. "Thank you for the water. I appreciate it. Is it ok with you if I talk to Alee for a few minutes before you two hang out?"

Mercy's heavy breathing backs off and Phil nods carelessly. "Sure, I'll grab a beer."

Taking Amberlee's arm gently, I pull her away from the bar and restaurant part of the club and into the women's bathroom.

As soon as the heavy gray door closes behind us, I lunge.

"What the hell is going on? Why did you come here last night after I told you to check into a hotel and what the fuck are you high on?"

"Face it, I don't have the protection you do. Being Dominic's girl, you're untouchable. I have no rank in this club, but I still need their protection, so I'm making sure Christian gives it to me."

"I don't trust Christian. What's to stop him from using you for sex, promising you protection, then not giving it to you when it's needed?"

"That's why I need to make sure I satisfy him and any of the other Serpents."

Staring into her bloodshot eyes, I feel a mixture of sympathy, anger, revulsion, and disappointment.

"So that's why you got high? So you can make it through fucking multiple men?"

"Well, you're killin' my buzz now. So..."

"So, what, you'll need to take more E or more cocaine? When does it end? When does the meaningless sex and drugs end?"

"I don't know!" she screams. "Ditch is threatening to kill me. I'm doing what I know to survive."

"Christian is taking advantage of you. He could give you the protection without you having to sleep with the Serpents. You already gave him the house and I know you're dealing drugs for him. You're never without them, but with Ditch being kicked out of the Serpents that caused problems with your clients. Whoever you dealt with before probably doesn't trust you now that Ditch is out. So now you're of no use to Christian except to be his plaything. Am I getting any of this right?"

Shock is written over her fragile face. Slow to catch everything I've said, she takes a moment to absorb it all. I know she has when her expression changes, her eyes glistening with tears.

"I'm in so deep, Erika. I don't know how to get out."

Pulling her into my arms, I rub her hair and back. She's lost weight. She feels so small against my chest.

"I'm going to help you. You're done giving yourself to the Serpents. You've given enough."

Pulling back from me, she wipes the stray tears from her cheeks. "What are you going to do?"

"Talk to Christian."

"Erika, wait." Grabbing my arm, she stops me from leaving. "Christian is conniving. His only concern is the Serpents. If you don't have anything to offer him, you're of no use to him."

CHAPTER SIXTEEN

ERIKA

PUSHING open Christian's office door, I catch him at the tail end of a phone call. He drops his cell phone on the desk and waves me in.

"Erika, what do you need?"

"To talk."

Brows furrowing, he sits back in his chair. "About what?"

"Amberlee."

Christian shrugs. "I don't think we need to talk about her. Your sister is a grown woman. She makes her own choices."

"Cut the bullshit. My sister's been backed into a corner, and she thinks the only way out is to fuck her way out which we both know is convenient for you and the Serpents. I'm here because my sister needs help. She's got a drug problem and she's terrified of Ditch coming after her. You probably don't give a shit what happens to her, but I do. She's the only family I've got. So yeah, we need to talk."

Sitting forward, he sets his elbows on the desk. "All right, Princess. What the fuck do you wanna talk about?"

"Let's start with my sister no longer being used as a fuck toy. She's paid her dues. You own our house and she's made you a lot of money dealing for you. You know she's scared of Ditch, so you're promising her protection in exchange for her putting out. That's low, Christian. She deserves your protection without having to sleep with everyone."

"You're a hell of a lot smarter than I gave you credit for," Christian laughs, casually sitting back in his chair.

"I'm pretty sure that's supposed to be a compliment, but you still sound like an ass."

Christian laughs harder, his hand wiping over his scruff. "Fuck, you're something." Standing, his boots thud on the floor, and my resolve weakens when he stands to his full height.

"I'm not sure what to do with you." Coming out from behind the desk, he stalks slowly toward me.

"You're demanding I be honorable and give your sister protection against one of my own brothers who I had to let go of *because* of you and your sister. Then you insult me and tell me how I should run my own club."

Hand to my throat, he places it there casually, then slowly his grip tightens as he backs me against the wall. Caged in by his body, his warm breath tickles my ear.

"You make me want to hurt you, to teach you a good, hard lesson, yet I'm beginning to respect you. You have more balls than some men I've seen enter this club. But the problem is I can't let you walk in here and think it's ok to demand things from me, not without giving me something in return."

Knowing what his marks on my neck will incite, I shove his hand off.

"Careful, Dominic doesn't like me being touched. And I'm not giving you shit. You already have my house. I'm just asking you to honor the deal you've already made."

Christian throws his hands up, mockingly.

"You wear his jacket well."

The door opens and Christian's gaze settles on the man entering. Mercy comes into view and I take a breath of relief. Evaluating the situation, Mercy quietly absorbs our body language.

"So, can I trust you to honor the deal you've already made? Or should I let Dom know you want something from me?"

Mercy's attention switches to Christian. Curiosity crosses his puckered brows.

"Our deal's good. Tell Alee to clean herself up," he replies, his jaw tight.

With the agitated look in his eyes, I have a worried feeling this isn't the end of this conversation.

Walking from Christian's office, Mercy tugs my jacket when we're a ways down the hall. "What the hell was that about? You shouldn't be making deals without Dom around. You in some kind of trouble with Christian?"

Looking behind us, I make sure no one is around. "No, Alee is. She made a deal with Christian that he isn't honoring. I just reminded him of the original deal he made. I'm trying to look out for my sister."

"I understand wanting to protect her, but you should let Dom handle things with Christian. You shouldn't have gone in there alone. You're in over your head, sweet thing."

Thundering engines are followed by a crash of glass. Mercy moves with sudden speed toward the bar and restaurant part of the club. In front of him, I see the shattered front window and the flaming bottle broken on the floor. Phil and another Serpent are already putting out the small fire. Christian and Amberlee join us from different directions of the clubhouse.

"The Jackals," Phil tells Christian. "They're sending a message. Gotta be from Dom's beef with Bronx."

Christian's gaze sweeps to me and his eyes narrow to slits. This isn't good.

Attention returning to the Serpents, Christian barks out orders. "Clean that shit up, then we're going on a ride."

Helping the Serpents clean the glass, I drop the last of it into a trash can with a broom. Returning it to its home behind the bar, I watch as Christian commands the Serpents to leave. Amberlee's been ordered to call and wait on someone to repair the window. I expect to be left with her, but Christian motions for me to join them.

"Dom wanted her kept away from business. You sure about her coming?" Mercy asks, a tinge of concern in his tone.

"Yeah, it's time the little Princess gets her hands dirty," Christian bites back.

Mercy reads my fearful expression and winks at me. "You'll ride with me. Ok?"

Nodding reluctantly, I hope he keeps his promise to Dominic.

Outside, I place my arms around Mercy's waist and hang on tight as the Serpents speed off. It's not long before we're pulling up to a light blue siding, two-story house along a common street. Christian steps off his bike, and I see the Glock he has tucked at the top of his black jeans. Climbing off Mercy's bike, I watch him reach into his saddlebag and pull his own gun. Eyes widening, Mercy steps in front of me, blocking my view of what's going on behind him.

"Whatever you see today, you'll need to forget. Got it?"

A thudding sound of a large body hitting a door sounds in the air followed by a woman screaming. Swallowing the lump in my throat, I nod to Mercy.

"Mercy! Get your ass up here."

Grabbing my jacket, he tugs me along with him. Inside, it's chaotic. There are two men and one woman.

They look like they were casually watching TV before we invaded their home. Against the wall, Christian has one of the men pinned, the Glock shoved under his chin.

"Tell me again. What are you going to tell the police?"

"That we lied. We didn't see shit," the man mutters, saliva pooling at the edge of his mouth.

I'm shoved into a corner before Mercy unleashes on the other guy the Serpents are holding up. With his arms held back by them, Mercy slams his fist into the guy's face, then his stomach, then repeats. Blood spatters from his mouth and nose as he heaves for each breath. The woman lunges for Mercy and I shout.

Mercy puts up an arm and she's clotheslined, knocked down to the floor, her breath cut from her momentarily. Tears fill my eyes as my mouth goes dry. Closing my eyes, I block out the horrific scene in front of me. As soon as my eyes shoot open, I rush out the front door. Back at Mercy's bike, I focus on my breathing. Slow deep breath in, slow deep breath out. Wiping the tears from my cheeks, I wish for Dominic. He would've kept me from this. It's Christian who wants me to see it. To see the dark side of the Serpents.

The four of them return to their bikes, wiping sweat and blood from their skin and clothes. My stomach is churning. I desperately want to be away from them. Mercy climbs on and I put my hands around his waist. Nothing is said as he pulls out and drives us to the next destination. The bikes come to a slow rumble as we approach a biker bar. I recognize the symbol on one of the saddlebags. The Jackals. Glock pulled from his waist, Christian fires, putting bullets into the bikes.

Shots echoing, I tighten my grip on Mercy's waist as fear seizes me. Men in colors come rushing from the building. Mercy takes off, and I look behind us, seeing the other bikes just behind us as I hear more gunshots.

My heart doesn't stop racing even after we've returned to the clubhouse. Mercy pries my fingers from his waist and guides me back inside. I'm in shock, everything around me a fuzzy blur. Seeing red hair and a red outfit, I know it's Amberlee. She's at the counter laughing with another woman.

Instead of joining her, I turn toward the entrance. I need out. I need to get away. I don't care if I have to walk back to Dominic's. I can't stay here.

"Mercy, bring her back," I hear Christian order behind me.

Amberlee and the woman stop laughing, their attention drawn in my direction.

Mercy blocks my exit. I stare up at him with pleading eyes. "I need to go."

Shaking his head, he puts his powerful hands on my shoulders and turns me to face Christian.

With his hand tight on my jaw, he raises my chin. "Those bullets are on you. Your whore of a mother brought a rival club member into *my* house. Dom had to handle it. So the Jackals thought they'd show some muscle today because of Bronx's busted up face. Which left us having to remind them who's king around here. And you, Princess, need to learn the same thing." I'm shoved back into Mercy's waiting arms. "Alee, why don't you give us all a show."

Cold, brown eyes fixed on mine, his smile is triumphant. The clubhouse door opens with more Serpents entering, Drake being one of them. The knot in my stomach tightens.

"Perfect timing, boys," Christian tells them. "Amberlee's about to dance for us."

Amberlee's expression hides her emotions as she fills a shot behind the counter, downs it and climbs atop the bar. Several men whistle at her, including Drake. Nausea fills my stomach. Yanking my arms from Mercy's, I head toward the double doors of their meeting room. Behind me, the sounds of music, whistles, and shouts fade into the distance as I pass through the doors.

Sitting in one of the chairs, tears stream down my face as I listen to the thudding of music and the shouts and whistles lessening. Behind me, one of the doors open and Mercy stops next to my chair.

"It's over."

"Where is she?"

"Drake took her to a room."

"What?!" Rising from the chair, I'm in a panic. I know what he'll do to her. I rush to go after them and Mercy grabs me.

"Stop this shit. All you're gonna do is piss off

Christian more. You don't have any rank in this club. The jacket earns you protection and respect. That's it. You don't have any say around here."

Turning on Mercy, I'm furious. "So I'm supposed to let Drake hurt her and do nothing about it? I've seen firsthand what he likes to do to women. I wouldn't be surprised if Christian is the one who suggested Drake take her to a room."

His head lowers and I know then, I'm right.

"My sister doesn't deserve to be treated like this. She's been nothing but loyal. It was Ditch who fucked up and now she's paying the price. If this is what it's like being a part of the Serpents," Shedding my jacket, I toss it at him. "Then I'm out. I'm taking Amberlee and we're leaving."

"You can't walk out," Mercy warns.

"Watch me."

Storming the halls, I search for the room. It doesn't take me long to hear their voices and Drake's grunts. Slamming the door open, I scream.

"Get the fuck off her!"

The tiny room isn't much more than a large storage closet with a small bed and a few furnishings. Drake pulls out of Amberlee, his face in a rage. Heat rises to my own when I see the red marks on her throat.

"Alee get dressed. We're leaving. Now!"

Eyes wide with fury, Drake tucks his cock back in his pants. He steps toward me, then stops abruptly, looking at the man behind me.

"Don't do it," I hear Mercy tell him. "Let them go."

Pulling her shorts up, Amberlee's expression is horrified and filled with fear. Grabbing her purse and keys, I take hold of her arm and stop in front of Mercy.

"Thank you," I mouth to him.

Moving to the side, he lets us go. In the clubhouse, everyone is occupied. We're barely noticed as I rush us out the door. Amberlee gets in the passenger side of her car as I start the engine of her Ford Taurus.

"Where we going?"

"Anywhere but here."

CHAPTER SEVENTEEN

DOMINIC

ENTERING THE CLUBHOUSE, I'm exhausted. Eight hours of bullshit questioning and being detained has taken its toll. I want to find my Sparrow, take her home, get a rub down, and lose myself inside of her. Seeing Mercy playing pool with Erika nowhere in sight has my muscles tightening. With a nod to him, he lowers his cue stick and licks his lips nervously. What the fuck is going on?

I clear the space between us in seconds. "Where is she?"

"She took off. She was pissed, brother. She left her jacket and took her sister. A lot of shit went down today you're not gonna like. We should go somewhere and talk."

Mercy gets to the end of everything he has to say and my fisted knuckles are white. Standing from the church table, I collect myself. I have to keep it together. I can only deal with one thing at a time and finding Erika is my first priority. Dealing with Christian can wait. I get he wants to put Erika in her place, but today he crossed the line. He disrespected me with every choice he made. And that will need to be dealt with.

"Shit, man, I don't know what got into Christian. I think your girl gets under his skin. Girl's got some nerve too. She didn't back down to him once. I think that's why he did the shit he did. He wanted to break her."

"He's playing some fucked up games over a bruised ego. She didn't need to see any of that shit today."

Worry is etched across Mercy's brows. "You goin' to talk to him now?"

"No. I need to cool down and find Erika. Thanks for keeping your word and looking after her."

"You know I got your back."

Taking Erika's jacket off the table, I head out. Securing her jacket in my saddle bag, I climb on and send her a text.

Where are you?

Her text comes back as I start the engine.

Your house.

Pulling into my driveway, I see Alee's car parked there. I'm not thrilled she's here. She causes Erika enough problems, but I didn't expect anything different either. I know how much Erika loves her sister and her loyalty runs deep, which was shown to me again.

Because of her, I have a solid alibi for the night I stabbed Carl. With the witnesses revoking their statements, the police no longer had anything to hold me on.

Walking through my back door, I see Alee rise from the couch with her drink and head upstairs. At least she knows to give us privacy. Turning off the TV, Erika stands from the couch, unease filling her beautiful hazel eyes as she looks at me and the jacket in my hand. Still, she comes to me, settling into my chest.

"Goddamn, I missed you, baby."

Voice cracked, I can tell she's fighting tears, "I missed you so much."

Tear-filled eyes look up at me as I pull back. "Let's go upstairs. We have a lot to talk about."

"Are you mad at me?"

Tossing her jacket on the back of the couch, I shake my head. "No, so don't worry about that."

"I made you dinner. I wanted you to have something good to eat when you got home."

"Thank you. Maybe I'll warm it up later. Right now, I want us in bed."

Taking her hand, I lead us upstairs. Behind my closed door, I pull her to me, kissing her like I've wanted to do for hours. Her warm lips melt to mine, full of passion and want.

"I can't wait any longer. I need to lose myself in you."

Soft, confidant hands snake up my abs, raising my shirt off. "That's all I want is to feel you."

Lifting her, her legs drape around my waist as I carry her to our bed. Laying her beneath me, I waste no time undressing us both. Legs tight over my hips, I thrust into her, and we both let out a breath of relief and satisfaction.

Clinging to me, her body arches, her lips parting, and sweet moans escape her mouth. There's nothing better. Nothing more free than the escape I get when fucking her. Riding hard against her pussy, I watch the pleasure fill her face, feel her walls tighten around my cock as she nears her orgasm.

"I'm gonna cum inside you, baby."

"Yes," she begs.

Raising her leg, I thrust hard and deep, filling her tight hole as I cum. Trembling beneath me, her pussy soaks my cock as she reaches her orgasm. Seeing her take pleasure from me like this, it does something to me, knowing I'm the only man to ever give it to her.

Lying above her, I can't stop kissing her, and I know she doesn't want me to stop either. Her legs are a vice grip on my ass, not letting me pull out of her. Caressing her cheek, I admire her subdued and loving expression.

"Today was rough for you, wasn't it? I can see it in your eyes."

Biting her lip, she releases her legs, and I pull out, turning us to our sides.

"Mercy told me everything that went on. I didn't

want you a part of any of that. Christian disrespected me with everything he did to you."

Reading my eyes, she pauses before speaking, "Dom, I hate him. He treats Alee horribly and doesn't treat me much better. I don't...want to go back there. I don't want to be a part of the Serpents."

Rolling onto my back, I absorb her words with a sting. The Serpents are my life. Always have been and now the woman I love—fuck, it's true, I love her—is telling me she doesn't want anything to do with them. Closing my eyes, I lay there wondering if this was part of Christian's game. Did he want her out? Did he want me to see her as weak by breaking her or push her to leave on her own?

"I'm sorry. I can tell you're upset, but seeing what I did today, how Alee and I were treated, I don't want any part of them."

"Did you strip your jacket in front of them?"

"No, only Mercy."

Her hand touches my chest, and I place my hand over it, needing to feel her, to calm the raging storm inside me.

"I asked Christian to honor his original agreement he made with Alee and to not use her as a fuck toy for the club members. He said he'd keep to the agreement and then later in the day, he made her strip for the club members and then gave her to Drake. He made his point clear to me. He doesn't give a shit about the deal or keeping his word."

"Enough."

Raising from the bed, I walk around it to take a shower. I need to clear my head and think things through.

"Are you going to break up with me or kick me out?" she asks, her voice breaking.

Turning to look at her, her eyes have welled up with tears. "I asked you not to ruin what we have, now you're asking me to choose between you and my family."

"Dom, that's not what I'm asking. I just...want to avoid them."

"Avoid us, Erika. I'm a Serpent. I'm a part of them."

The pain in her eyes is unbearable. Turning away from her, I enter the bathroom, stopping at the doorway. "Don't leave. I want you here when I get out."

The heat of the water running down my back does little to settle my emotions. I'm pissed. This day went to shit real fucking fast. All I wanted was for my brothers to protect her while I was being detained. Instead, Christian played mind games with her all day to the point she's scared of us. I know that's what that fucker wanted, for her to yield or walk away. I never want her to yield to him, respect him, yes, yield, never, but I can't let her walk away either. She needs to choose me over her fear. She should know I'll do anything to protect her. She shouldn't be giving me an ultimatum. It's her who needs to decide. If she's loyal to me, she has to be loyal to the Serpents. There's no other way.

Stepping out of the shower, I see her birth control,

toothbrush, and makeup is gone. Muscles tightening, my anger rises. When I heard her in here, I didn't expect she was packing her shit up. Towel wrapped around my waist, I look into our room. Sure as shit, she has her bag packed and on the bed, ready to go.

"What are you doing?"

Placing her bathroom bag in her duffle, she doesn't look my way. "I'm not making you choose between me and them. I already know where I stand. I've seen this before. I'm not going to go through it."

"What are you talking about?"

Turning to face me, her eyes are red and swollen. She's been crying the entire time I've been in the shower.

"I think Christian's hatred is deeper than you realize. My father was a Jackal before he was stripped of his colors. Christian knows that, and with my father gone, somehow, my family has become Christian's to abuse. I'm a problem for him because I'm of no use to him nor will I submit to him. I won't ever give myself sexually, I won't ever deal drugs for him, I won't ever respect him after today. I love you, Dom, more than I thought was possible to love someone, but I saw the fights my parents had. My father always chose the Jackals over her. She hated him for it. I don't want to become them. It's better I make the choice for us and get out of your life now before I ruin it."

Her words are a blade cutting through my chest. I

need to get this situation under control now. There's no way in hell she's leaving.

Grabbing a pair of jeans, I pull them on as she puts the last of her things in her bag. "You didn't tell me about your father."

"Because I'm more than my father's daughter. I'm going to get out of this town and make a life for myself. One where no one knows my family and the horrible shit my last name carries."

Reaching for her, she backs away. That incites me further.

"Erika." Taking her in my arms, I force her against me. Tears collect in her eyes. "You're not leaving me. Get that thought out of your fucking head, now. I want you with me. I *need* you. I know you feel the same or you wouldn't be hurting like you are. Leaving isn't an option. I won't let you."

Expecting a fight, my arms tighten, but she doesn't resist. Deep down, she doesn't want to go, and that gives me relief.

"You want to stay, don't you?"

"It's better if I don't."

Hand fisted in her long, soft hair, I pull it back, bringing her broken gaze to mine.

"So, what's your plan then? Go back home, forget about me? You think you can do that?"

"No, I could never forget about you."

Tears line the edges of her eyes. Backing her to the bed, I put her beneath me on the mattress, her reddish-brown hair splaying out behind her beautiful face. Taking her hands in mine, I raise them above her head as I claim her mouth, sliding my tongue between her lips, drawing her need for me to the front of her mind.

"I'd never let you."

Thrusting against her, she moans below me.

"You're mine, Sparrow. Don't ever forget that."

"Dom..." she calls into my ear, her voice needy with desire.

"Tell me you love me."

"I love you," she promises.

Another thrust and she cries out in pleasure.

"Tell me you want me."

"I want you more than anything."

My lips to hers, I unbutton her jeans, then slide them from her hips.

"If you want me, then you don't walk away when things get rough." Removing her jeans and underwear, I step between her legs, rubbing her clit beneath my thumb. "You turn to me when you're afraid."

Sliding two fingers into her wet opening, her breath catches. "I won't abandon you because I'm a Serpent."

Unzipping my jeans, I reach between and pull out my erection. Pulling her to the edge of the bed, I tease her swollen pussy lips with my tip.

"Trust me, baby. Trust me to protect you."

Thrusting into her, she cries out in satisfaction. Holding the crease of her thighs, I slam into her, fucking her hard, claiming what's mine.

I never want her to forget what it feels like to have me inside her. To own every ounce of her loyalty and her love. She'll always be mine, and tonight, I'll do what it takes to remind her of that.

CURLED IN MY ARM, her hair fans across my chest, her fingers intertwined with mine. Raising our joined hands, I kiss her fingers.

"Do you love me?" her voice sounds soft, hopeful.

"If you were any other woman, I would've let you walk out."

"Dom."

Raising her chin, I look into her emotion filled eyes. "Yes. I love you." Taking her lips, I seal my words with a kiss. Putting her hand on my face, she keeps it going, expressing her love with each passionate movement of her lips.

"I'm sorry for packing my things. For saying I was leaving."

"I knew you wouldn't go. You don't want to. The things Christian did to you today scared you, I understand that, but you should've known I'll handle it." Rubbing her arm, her eyes close momentarily, enjoying the feel of my caress. "If you want to be with me, you need to accept all of me, even the darkest parts. But know I'll protect you from that part of my life."

"I do accept all of you. I was willing to accept the

Serpents too. Christian took it too far. He changed my mind."

"Baby, that's what he wanted. He wanted you to submit to him or walk away from the Serpents. It's the same way he treats every new prospect or hang around. But I'd never ask you to submit to him. I don't expect that. You're mine, not his. That's something I'll work out with him on my own time. As for avoiding the Serpents, you can't. There's gonna be times I want you to ride with me, come to the clubhouse or a party. If you're with me, you know you have nothing to be afraid of, don't you?"

Uneasiness tightens her face. "I don't ever want to be left alone with them, Dom. I'm afraid of your brothers."

Taking her face in my hand, I stare into her eyes, intent on dissolving the fear I see in them.

"I'd never let anyone hurt you that includes my brothers."

Kissing me, a smile skirts her lips. "I want you to know I trust you, completely."

"I know you do. That means something to me, so does the loyalty you showed me today."

Hand caressing my chest, she stares up at me with absolute devotion.

"I want to protect you just like you want to protect me. I don't want anything to happen to you. If something did, Dom, I'd fall apart."

Something unfamiliar constricts my chest. For the

first time in my life, I have a reason to be careful because I now have something to lose.

Pulling her to me, I lay her above me and let the day's events slip away as I caress between her legs, my lips greedily kissing hers.

CHAPTER EIGHTEEN

DOMINIC

Entering the clubhouse, it looks like they're partying hard tonight, ending the weekend strong. Not long ago, I would've enjoyed the women drawn to it, but no clubhouse slut compares to Erika's pussy. I feel drugged every time my cock's inside her and I can't get enough. She's my addiction and my salvation. She's opened my blackened heart and given me something more to live for. She sees me as her protector, the man to take care of her, and she's right, I am.

With a sweep of the place, I don't see Christian which means he's in his office probably getting laid. Several brothers chat me up and let me know they're glad to see me. I keep the conversations short as I work my way through the room. Getting to the bar, I take a shot of whiskey before heading to Christian's office.

As I reach the door, I know a woman's inside with

him by the moaning and groaning sounds I hear. Opening it, I see the familiar bleach blond hair on Roxy's head as she bobs up and down on Christian's cock.

"That's it, bitch. Take all my cum."

Cleaning him off, she pulls back and looks up at me with her long, dark lashes and grins.

"Hey, Dom. You wanna join?"

"Nah, Rox, he's hooked on some virgin tail. Hasn't had another woman since," he tells her, tucking his dick back in his jeans.

Roxy laughs, wiping her mouth. "Well, she's not a virgin anymore now that Dom's had her. I'm sure he's tore that pussy up good."

"Careful, Rox, he's a bit sensitive about her," he mocks.

In a short, black skirt and too high of heels, she moves around his desk toward the door. As she passes she reaches between my legs, rubbing my cock.

"That's too bad. Having both of you fuck me at once was a hell of a lot of fun."

With a kiss on my cheek, she saunters out.

The door closes and Christian smirks.

"See what you're missing?"

"I'm not missing shit. That was a one and done. Erika fucks better than that cunt."

"Her pussy must be something to have you wrapped around her finger like she does."

"What's your problem with her?" I cut to the point.

Shrugging carelessly, he leans against the front of his desk. "I don't have a problem with her, it's the problems she causes."

"Problems *she* causes. From my perspective, she's helped you out. Her whole family has. Buying her house moved you farther into the Jackal's turf. You never do anything without reason. Now I know why you jumped on that deal with Alee. Convenient deal you got out of it too. Not just moving into the Jackal turf, but you gained more clients, got a stash house, then when Ditch fucked up, you got a sex toy for the club members. Tell me again how my girl is causing you problems."

Thumbs in his vest, he scoffs. "Maybe I'm looking at it differently. My closest brother's been distant lately. More occupied with Erika's pussy than the club. We lost Ditch because of her and her sister. And now we're in a retaliation war because her trash mother brought a rival club member into my house and you had to handle it. Add in, you fucking up Drake's face because he was playing around with her."

Arms crossed, I glare back at him, heat rising up my neck. "Let's back this up. Drake and Ditch are problems themselves. Ditch needed to go and I don't know why the hell you're still hanging onto that. In my eyes, the girls did us a favor before he cost us clients, or worse, a bullet in one of the members. Drake and Ditch tried to make a move on what's mine. You expect me to let that shit fly? I know you don't, so I don't want to hear any more about it. I've been committed to this club more than any other member. So I found a woman to satisfy me. Get the fuck over it. I'm still here, aren't I? Still takin' care of business? As for Bronx, that was a mistake of her mother's. The woman is so drugged out, she doesn't know what the hell she's doing. You can't bitch too much about that when you're the one supplying her."

Licking his lips, Christian lets the bottom lip slide from his teeth.

"Yesterday, you were supposed to protect her, not humiliate and scare the shit out of her. You disrespected me, brother. In a way I'm having trouble dealing with."

Eyes meeting mine, they narrow. "If she wants to be a part of the Serpents, then she needs to know what it takes and learn to respect the hierarchy."

"You mean respect you. She already respected the Serpents, it was you she didn't trust. Seeing the way you treated her sister and the shit you put her through, she lost that respect. Your plan to make her submit or walk didn't work. She didn't back down to you and she didn't leave me either. She's a hell of a lot tougher than you give her credit for."

"She's the daughter of a traitorous drug dealer and murderer. You're giving her too much credit."

Closing in, my muscles bulge. "She's more than her father's daughter. She's mine. She's an extension of me. Keep disrespecting her and I'll see it as disrespect to me. This is the last time we're having a conversation about this."

Turning from him, I pace to the door.

"Have her make a commitment to us publicly at the next party and I'll drop it."

Looking over my shoulder, I deadpan.

"Don't push me, Christian."

CHAPTER NINETEEN

ERIKA

SHOVING Amberlee's car door closed, I try to stop her from leaving. "You shouldn't go if you're worried about Ditch coming after you."

"I need to. I can't stay here."

"You need a fix. That's why you're really leaving. You're restless, bored. You want to party, fuck, and get high."

"Well, I can't sit around and play Susie homemaker to Dom. You've already taken that job."

Before she rushed out the back door saying she was leaving, I was making us all dinner. It's a low jab she's making, but I know it's the mood swings, the irritability of withdrawal.

"Let me take you to the hospital. They can get you clean. You won't have to struggle through the withdrawals. Please, Alee. Do it for me."

Amberlee's tired eyes look over my shoulder as Dominic's motorcycle rumbles behind us.

"I'll go. I'll drive myself. I promise. You don't need to babysit me. You need to be here for Dom. He doesn't look happy."

She's right. Turning, I see the brooding mood written on his face, but whatever it is, it can wait. I want to help her. She doesn't have to face this by herself.

"I still want to come with you. You don't have to go alone."

"You're a good sister, you know that?" Hugging me, she squeezes me tight. "I love you." Quickly, she opens the car door and jumps in. "Take care of Dom. I'll call you later."

"Alee!"

Looking ahead, she ignores my plea. Frustration builds, putting a knot in my gut as her car disappears into the night.

"Baby, what's wrong?"

"She needs help." Collapsing into his chest, the tears flow. "I wanted to take her to the hospital, to help her get clean. She insisted on going alone. I don't believe she'll go."

Wiping the tears from my cheeks, his sympathetic expression and warm touch are already working to soothe me.

"She probably won't. The fix is more important to her."

"I should go after her."

"To where? Where do you think she went?"

"Home. She probably has drugs there."

"I'll take you. You're not going there without me."

After putting food away and locking up the house, I climb on his Harley behind him. Crossing to the other side of town, Dominic pulls up the driveway to my old house. Amberlee's car is here and relief washes over me. In the distance, we hear the rumble of motorcycles and Dominic goes on high alert. Pulling a pistol from his saddlebag, he puts it under his jacket at the top of his jeans. Arm around me, he scans our surroundings as we head to the door.

"We can't be here long, ok?"

"Ok."

Entering, the house is quiet. Unusually quiet. I flick on the living room lamp and see there's been a tussle. Broken glass is scattered across the floor and the chair is toppled over.

"Dori! Alee!"

Rushing to Amberlee's room, I find it empty.

"Dom, where is she?"

"I don't know. Baby, we need to go. Something's not right."

Tears fill my eyes. "Those motorcycles. You think she left with them?"

Dominic grips my arm, not enough to hurt me, but enough to get my attention.

"There's fresh blood on the floor. We need to go. Now."

Crossing back over town, I immediately jump off his bike and dial Amberlee as soon as he parks. Her phone goes to voicemail.

"She's not answering. Oh God, Dom, do you think Ditch took her?"

"Sparrow, look at me." Taking my wrists, he tries to keep me focused as I lose my composure. "I'll make some calls inside. I don't know what's going on, but I'll try to find out."

Pacing in his living room, I call Amberlee repeatedly. Each call going to voicemail like the last. In the kitchen, he's leaned against the counter on his phone. Hanging up, his expression is menacing.

"What's wrong?"

"Drake and Levi are MIA. They left the clubhouse together a couple hours ago. Can't get a hold of them now."

My heartbeat pounds in my ears as my knees weaken. Dominic is there instantly, his strong arms holding me up. Easing me to the couch, he pulls me onto his lap and holds me as I sob into his chest.

"What are they going to do to her?"

"Ssh, baby, I'm sorry."

COMING OUT OF RESTLESS SLEEP, I sit up and take a sip

from the whiskey glass on the coffee table. Stirred awake, Dominic caresses my head and hair. My eyes are swollen from crying, my muscles sore from falling asleep on the couch. Checking my phone like I've done every hour or two, there are still no calls from Amberlee. Scooping his arms under my legs and around my back, Dominic lifts me from the couch.

"I'm taking you to bed. I'll make a couple calls, then join you."

Burying my head in his shoulder, I cling to him as he carries me up the stairs. Fresh tears roll down the side of my face as he lays me on the mattress.

"Do you think they killed her?"

Silence fills the room, a heavy darkness sucking the life out of it.

"Get some rest. I'll be up in a little while."

His warm hand caresses my back. As he walks out the door, I give into more uncontrollable sobs.

PHONE RINGING, I jump awake, unsure of the time or how long I've been asleep. Next to me, Dominic sits up, reaching for my phone.

"Alee, where are you?"

Hope fills my chest. She's alive.

"We're on our way."

Hanging up, he tosses the phone on the bed as he quickly stands and finds clothes.

"Where is she?"

"Your old house. She needs taken to the hospital."

More tears fill my eyes as I rush to put on pants. When I reach the bottom of the steps, Dominic already has his boots and jacket on. Stumbling through the tiredness, I put my own on as quickly as I can.

The clock on Dominic's Camaro reads three thirty-six a.m. Behind the wheel, his expression is hardened and focused on the road as he speeds through the night. With Dori not arriving home until nine a.m., it kills me knowing Amberlee is suffering alone. By the time Dominic reaches my old house, the knot in my stomach is agonizingly painful.

"Dom, I'm afraid. I'm afraid of what I'll see."

"Stay in the car."

He's out and to the front door in seconds, disappearing inside. I hold my breath for what's coming. Carrying Amberlee in his arms, he brings her to the car. I rush out, opening the door for him to put her in the back. She's wrapped in a blanket, barely conscious. I can't see what's been done to her body, but her one eye is swollen shut. Severe bruising and dried blood cover her cheek and jaw.

Running back to the passenger seat, I hold Amberlee's hand as Dominic speeds to the nearest hospital. Once parked, Dominic strips his Serpent jacket, leaving it in the driver seat before going to the back to get Amberlee. I do the same, leaving my jacket in the car and follow him into the emergency room.

Moments after arriving and demanding help, nurses bring a wheelchair and Amberlee is placed into it and whisked away.

Sitting in the lobby, I do my best to stay composed and fill out paperwork. After it's completed, and more agonizing waiting, they finally let me go to the room she's in. Under a hospital blanket, she's asleep, an IV attached to her.

Behind me, a short, curvy female doctor walks in. On her light chocolate round face is an empathetic expression.

"Are you her sister? The one who brought her in?"

"Yes. Is she going to be ok?"

"She has a concussion, two broken ribs, and lacerations across her body. Your sister said she was sexually assaulted by multiple men. The police are going to want to speak with you and her, so please wait for them here. If either of you need anything, press this button. There's also a security guard on this floor. You're both safe here."

Maybe it's the fear and exhaustion on my face that has her saying those things. Maybe it's standard protocol. Either way, it's comforting.

"Thank you."

The doctor steps out and I collapse into the nearest chair. Taking my phone from my pocket, I text Dominic.

Thank you for helping us. I'm going to stay with Alee. You don't have to wait. Go home and get some sleep. I love you.

Come to the lobby. I need to see you before I go.

Coming off the elevator, I enter the lobby and see Dominic rise from a chair. Throwing myself into his arms, I fight the urge to break down. As if he senses it, he caresses my hair and back.

"I'll stay if you want me to."

"No," I shake my head, wiping the tears from my eyes. "I want you to get some sleep. I'll need you when I leave here."

Stroking my face, he holds me close. "As soon as you're ready to leave, call me. I'll drop what I'm doing and come get you."

"Thank you. I miss you already."

"I'm gonna miss you today too." Hugging me, he eases back and raises my chin, kissing me. "I love you."

CHAPTER TWENTY

ERIKA

IT'S BEEN two days since Amberlee was brought to the hospital. Being released today, I've made sure to be there for her. All paperwork signed, I hold Amberlee steady as she stands from the hospital bed. She's asked for privacy to change her clothes. I'm the only one she wants around.

With a grimace, she takes each step to the bathroom. Inside, she leans against the sink counter and looks in the mirror. Sobs break from her chest when she sees her black eye, bruised jaw, and the marks on her neck. Enclosing my arms around her, I hold her as she cries into my shoulder.

"I'm so sorry."

"The things they did to me."

With her tears soaking my shirt, I hold her against me, broken inside. She's my sister, my family, the one who's always looked out for me, and those animals tortured her. Two of them are still Serpents and Dom knows this is a problem for me.

Minutes pass before she's able to stop crying. Wiping the tears from her cheeks, I look into her eyes. The woman looking back at me is shattered. She's a shell of the sister I know. Seeing her like this, broken down to her core, hurting physically, mentally, emotionally, it's cutting me raw.

Letting the hospital gown drop to her folded arms, she clutches it at her breasts as more tears fall from her eyes. With her naked in front of me, I fight back sobs. Bruises cover her entire body; neck, upper arms, torso, butt, and thighs. Cigarette burn marks scorched the skin of her breasts. Cuts from a blade have left lacerations on her right arm, side, and thigh. They'll be scars from those cuts, they're too deep not to. They wanted her to suffer and she did in the most horrible way possible. Clenching my teeth, anger rips through me, blackening my heart. I want those fuckers to pay. Somehow, I'll make them pay.

STEPPING through the door of my old home, it's an odd detached feeling. I grew up in this home, but I feel no warmth, no love entering it. It's four walls containing far too many heartbreaking memories. I don't want my sister to remember the night of her attack every time she walks in here either which is why I've found a place for her and Dori to rent. They need out from under Christian's thumb. With that freedom, they can begin recovering from their addictions and Amberlee from her physical and emotional wounds.

I'm concerned for her. It's been a week since being released from the hospital and she's become distant. No matter how I've approached the subject, she won't talk about what happened. Attempts to get her out of the house have been unsuccessful, so I keep coming over, making her lunch, cleaning the house, anything to spend time with her and help her.

Placing the warm roast beef sandwich on a plate, I grab a fork and knife and bring them to her on the couch.

"I found a place for rent. Will you come with me tomorrow to look at it? It'd be a great place for you and Dori."

Tired eyes search my face. "Yeah, I'll come."

I'm shocked by her response. I didn't expect it. Smiling, I return to the kitchen for my own sandwich. Sitting next to her, I look at the TV, but I don't care what's on it.

"I can pick you up tomorrow morning after Dori gets home. It'd be nice if she came too."

Swallowing her bite, she nods. "I'll talk to her."

It's a small victory, but I'll take it. Maybe she's ready to leave this place.

"How's things with you and Dom?"

Her question surprises me. "Complicated," I reply

honestly. "Two of the men who hurt you are his brothers. He has his own feelings about what happened, and it's been hard on him."

Looking over at her, her eyes are glistening with oncoming tears.

"Don't go near them. I never should've."

"You should talk about it, to someone, it doesn't have to be me. The doctor said there are therapists."

"Stop." Setting her fork down on her plate, she moves the plate to the coffee table. "I'm tired. I don't wanna talk."

Bracing her hand on the arm of the couch, she struggles to stand. I rise to help and she waves me off.

My gut tightens when she enters the kitchen and pulls the cap from a liquor bottle. Without a cup, she puts the bottle to her lips and takes several swallows. I see it even if she doesn't. She's locked inside herself, hiding from the pain with alcohol and drugs.

"Alee, that's not going to fix it. It's a band-aid. When you're sober, the pain will come back."

"Maybe if you'd stop reminding me every damn time you come over."

"I want to help you. I hate seeing you like this."

"What do you want to hear? That I'll talk someone? Tell a complete stranger about how I was gang raped, had a knife cut into me, fell in and out of consciousness while I was tortured and sodomized by more than one man at a time."

Swallowing the knot in my throat, I watch Alee walk

to her room, the bottle dangling from her hand. Stopping at the doorway, she doesn't look at me.

"You should go. It's not safe for you to keep coming over. Don't come back."

The door shuts behind her and I drop to the couch, my head falling into my hands as I cry into them.

CHAPTER TWENTY-ONE

DOMINIC

Tapping on my shoulder, Mercy says what he can to keep me from losing my temper and breaking every bone in Drake and Levi's face.

"C'mon, Dom. Keep it cool."

They've been avoiding the clubhouse all week, but they couldn't avoid the church meeting. Christian had club business to go over and at the end of the meeting, I took the opportunity to mention what fucking cockroaches they are.

"Oh c'mon, Dom, the bitch asked for it. So we roughed her up a bit. We didn't kill her."

"I carried her limp body into the hospital. The girl didn't deserve to be tortured like that."

Christian's eyes sweep across either side of the Serpent table, taking in the heated argument.

"What'd you expect, boys? That's his ol' lady's sister. You shouldn't of tore her up like that. We all enjoyed having her around. She was a good fuck. She's not gonna come around now."

Drake shrugs. "So things might'a got out of hand. We were caught up in the moment. What's done is done."

His careless attitude fuels the fire already blazing inside of me.

"I want a fight night. Cage fight...in the ring. Hell, I'll take both of you fuckers on at the same time. Give you a taste of how I like to get *caught up in the moment*."

A few of the brothers grin at that. Their gazes move to Christian, anxiously awaiting his response.

"I'll allow it," Christian replies. "This shit needs to be worked out, then put to rest."

Expressions downcast, Drake and Levi look to one another. I can see the fear in their eyes.

"I want it tomorrow night," I demand.

With a tilt of his head, Christian accepts. "Get ready for a hell of a show, boys," he tells the members. "Church is dismissed."

The members clear out of the room except the board; Christian, myself, our treasurer Mike, secretary Sam, Road Captain John, and Sergeant at Arms Mercy.

"We need to talk about those two," Mercy presses. "There's gonna be heat on us if she talks to the police. If she hasn't already."

"She hasn't," I inform them. "She's too scared to, but that doesn't let them off the hook. They're a problem. Their loyalties are more aligned with their clique of brothers than the club. They're still runnin' with Ditch. I want to bring it to vote whether or not we should strip them of their colors."

Sitting back in his chair, Christian's thumb and forefinger rest on his chin as he observes me. "You don't think fight night and a suspension of colors is enough?"

"Fuck, no, I don't. This won't be a lesson learned for them. It'll be a lesson on how to hide their actions better."

"I agree with Dom," Mercy tips his head. "They're not respecting the patch. The fact they're running with Ditch after he was stripped of his colors rubs me the wrong way."

With a sigh, Christian sits forward. "All right, we'll vote. Those who feel Drake and Levi should be given a beating and their colors suspended, say Aye."

Christian, Mike, and Sam raise their hands and say Aye. Seeing Christian's choice to vote against me is like a whip slashing across my skin—it's a fierce sting.

"Those who feel Drake and Levi should be given a beating and stripped of their colors, say Aye."

Myself, John, and Mercy raise our hands and say Aye.

"We're at a draw, brothers. Drake and Levi will face fight night, suspension of their colors, and be put on a probationary period. We'll vote again after the probationary period ends. Acceptable?"

My brothers all nod, except me, but it doesn't

matter, that's how it's handled in the Serpents when there's a draw.

The rest of the board head out except Christian and me. Walking to the cooler, I pull out a beer and pop the top.

"You didn't see what I did, Christian. They brutally raped and beat her. She's not coming back from that and it's killing Erika and that's fucking with me."

"You love this girl?"

"What do you think?"

"I think you do and it's messing with your judgment. If not for her, we wouldn't be talking about stripping their colors, would we?"

Dropping back into the chair, I stare him down.

"Their actions have become my problems. That's what we're talking about. I'm the one who had to stay up all night with Erika, afraid her sister had been killed, and I'm the one who went out at three thirty in the morning to take a battered woman to the hospital. That girl didn't deserve what was done to her. All she wanted was for Ditch to stop treating her like a fucking punching bag. Now I see you defending them against me. How do you think I should feel about that?"

Dark, brown eyes stare boldly back at me.

"You're not the only one I have to think about, Dom. I have sixteen other members. If I let Drake and Levi go, what's to stop them from joining the Jackals or Black Diamonds? Why let them go when I can easily rein them in?"

"Strength in numbers. That's what's important to you?" Standing, I set the beer bottle on the table. "What about the brotherhood? What about protecting the family and the women in it? Or has the money, drugs, and turf war become so important, we're turning a blind eye to brothers raping and maiming Serpent women? I can't even bring my girl into this clubhouse without having to keep my eyes on her at all times. Maybe you need to think about that."

CHAPTER TWENTY-TWO

ERIKA

DOMINIC WALKS through the back door and as soon as I see him my heart leaps. Going to him, I take immense pleasure in the feel of his arms around me, cocooning me against his broad, hard chest. Raising my chin, he kisses me, and the stress of the day eases from my shoulders. When he lifts my ass, I put my legs around his toned waist. Sitting me on the counter, he pushes forward between my legs, teasing me with his hardening bulge.

Raising my shirt over my head, he licks and sucks my breasts. Pulling the fabric of my bra back, my nipple pops free, and he sucks it into his mouth. Hand through his hair, I tug as my pleasure increases, heat building between my legs.

The cool air tickles my nipple when his mouth leaves it. With a devilish grin, he tugs at my shorts, wiggling them and my underwear off my hips and legs.

Reaching down, I pull his button and zipper as his tongue invades my mouth. Folding his jeans off his hips, I reach into his briefs and pull his erection out. His lips never leave mine as he slides his cock into me.

Pulling me to the edge of the counter, his strong arms hold me there, teetering me on the lip as he thrusts in and out, making me moan in sexual bliss.

"Fuck, baby, your pussy's just what I needed."

"Harder. Take me harder."

He pulls out, dropping my legs and turns my ass to face him. Arms gripping the counter, he pushes into me, and I nearly come then. Hand wound through my hair, my back arches as he grips my hip, pounding into me.

My breath catches when he releases my hair, grabs my legs, and raises them off the floor. With my legs over his arms, he slams my pussy down onto his cock again and again and I come hard, half moaning, half pleasure screaming through my release. His thrusting slows as he reaches his own release.

"Lean back against me."

I do, and he lets my legs down and slides his hands up and around my chest as my feet touch the floor. His free hand turns my head to kiss him.

"You satisfy me like no other pussy can."

"Good. I want my pussy to be the only pussy you ever want."

Chuckling, he kisses me. "It already is."

Turning in his arms, I lock my lips to his, needy for more of his touch, more contact between us. It's the only time in this last week I've been able to forget everything else.

"Take me upstairs. Make love to me."

Lifting me, a smile skims his lips before he kisses me again.

"I love how greedy your pussy is for my cock."

"Always."

Lips feathering mine, he nibbles my bottom lip. "I love you, baby, so fucking much."

IN ONE OF his white tank tops and my underwear shorts, I finish cooking us dinner. In nothing but worn, ripped jeans and sexy black ink, he's leaning against the counter watching me, admiring me while I prepare our plates.

"How did it go with Alee?"

Remembering the last words she said to me, I stop prepping the plates and bite my lip as tears well up in my eyes. Strong hands caress my arms before his warm chest meets my back.

"I'm sorry you and your sister are hurting the way you are. I promise to make Drake and Levi suffer. I'm fighting them tomorrow night. I'll hurt them. I'll make them pay for what they did to you both."

Hearing his promise, I break, the emotions pouring out of me in tears. He holds me through it, kissing my head and cheek.

"Let it out, baby. I know you've been hurting and keeping it in."

Turning in his arms, I cry against his chest. It's the first I've broken down in front of him. Since Amberlee's assault, I've only cried when I was alone.

"You're fighting them at the clubhouse?"

Wiping my tears with his hands, his beautiful green eyes look into mine. In them, I see affection mixed with a fierce determination.

"Yes. It'll be a cage fight. Me against them. I won't let them go out quickly."

"Can I watch?"

A proud smile raises the corner of his mouth.

"Yes, but I want you to stay with Mercy. Don't leave his side. No matter what."

"I won't."

"Have you ever handled a gun?"

The question surprises me. "Yes."

"Your father teach you?"

"Yeah."

"Any good with it?"

"If you're wondering if I can shoot the target I'm aiming at, the answer is yes."

"What about a man? That's different."

"I don't know."

"I want you to start carrying one. We'll go to a range. Make sure you're comfortable handling it."

"Why do you want me to start carrying one?"

"Because, baby, I'm going to fuck them up, and their

egos won't let them take that kind of beating without having a grudge against me. I want you protected when I'm not with you."

Worry constricts my chest.

"Maybe...you shouldn't fight them. I don't want you to have to watch your back all the time."

"I won't be watching my back, my true brothers will. One wrong step and I won't hesitate to put them down." Caressing my face, his half smile is reassuring. "Don't worry about me, ok. Let's have dinner." Carrying the plates into the living room, he sets them on the coffee table. When I enter, he pulls me into his lap.

"We'll eat in here. I want you in my arms all night."

CHAPTER TWENTY-THREE

ERIKA

EVEN WITH AMBERLEE'S demand for me to stay away, I can't. I made the appointment with the landlord of the rental property for a visit and I'm keeping it. Not only that, she's in a dark place. She needs me even if she doesn't want me around. Pulling up the drive, her car is there just as I expected. Dori's is gone as I also expected. Whether Amberlee talked to Dori about the new place to rent or not, I don't know. She hasn't answered any of my calls today.

Opening the front door, I'm accosted by the sound of running water. I quickly run into the kitchen, stepping through a pool of water and turn off the faucet.

"Alee!"

She doesn't call back. I head to her room to find her. When I open the door, I'm relieved to find her there asleep on her side.

"Alee, you left the sink running."

She doesn't stir, which is normal. She's a heavy sleeper. Climbing across the bed, I join her. Rubbing her arm to wake her, my body tightens. Her skin feels cool and damp. With a shaky hand, I turn her toward me. Gagging, I fight back nausea when I see the blood and vomit spilled from her mouth across the pillow and blanket. Lifeless golden hazel eyes stare up at the ceiling. Hands trembling, I reach for my phone as my eyes become wet with tears.

"911, what's your emergency?"

"520 Lumont Street. My sister has overdosed."

"I'm dispatching a paramedic to you now."

Several questions later, I hang up, trembling, losing control, waiting for the ambulance to arrive. I hear the sirens in the distance and rush to the door to make sure it's unlocked. Waving them in, I point them to her room. Collapsing on the floor, my head falls into my arms as I listen to them administer medical attention. Moments later, she's rushed to the ambulance on a stretcher.

The ambulance pulls out and I hurry to Dominic's Camaro. With my trembling hands, I'm unable to start the car. The keys drop, and I completely break down, sobbing into the steering wheel. Forcing slow deep breaths, I lift the phone and dial my mother.

"It better be important."

"Alee, the ambulance took her to the hospital. She overdosed."

The line goes silent for several beats.

"I'll get off work. I'll be there." I can hear the fear in her tone.

My next call is to Dom, but it goes to voicemail.

"I'm going to the hospital. Alee overdosed. Please call me as soon as you can. I need you."

With more slow, deep breaths, I collect my composure enough to drive. Fear is a tight ball in my gut the entire way to the hospital. The image of Amberlee lingers in my mind, plaguing me, churning the nausea in my stomach with the memory.

Pulling into the emergency parking area, I run inside. I'm the first to get there, I don't see my mother. A nurse pulls me aside and the look on her face begins the horrific conversation that comes next.

Amberlee is dead. Dead on arrival.

The next moments are a blur. I don't remember much of the people who spoke to me, what they said, or what I said in return. All I remember is minutes later seeing Dominic walk through the sliding glass doors and his muscular figure lifting me into his arms.

"Erika."

My swollen eyes blink a couple times before Dominic comes into focus. We're at his house, on his couch. I'm in his arms. The memories come rushing back and I sob against his chest.

"She's gone."

Holding me tight against him, he kisses my head.

"I know, baby. I'm so sorry."

"Will you take me to my old house? I want to see Dori and..."

"Alee isn't there."

More sobs break free. "I don't want to accept it. I want to go over there. I want to talk to her, to hug her. Dom, I can't. I can't do this. I'm not strong like you are."

Putting my face in both his hands, he looks me in the eyes, his own full of pain. "Yes, you are. Don't ever doubt that. I know you're hurting. I've been there. I've felt every agonizing pain you're feeling now. I'll be here for you. I'll listen. I'll hold you. You *will* get through it. The pain will lessen, but you'll remember her. Always remember her."

Gently bringing my face to his, he kisses me tenderly. So soft, so caringly, my tears of grief mix with tears of appreciation.

More composed, I put my hand in his as his free hand rubs along my arm and back.

"It happened so fast. I'm still—"

"In shock."

"Yes. I don't want to accept she won't be at home when I go over there. I want her to be there. I want to talk to her. I want to hug her. I want to fix her and make her better."

"I know. It's the hardest part."

"How did you do it?"

"I shut myself off from feeling. I fucked, drank, fought, rode for hours, maybe days. It's all a blur. I don't want to see you do that. I want you to come to me when you need me."

"I love you."

"I love you too." Firm hand caressing me, he soothes me with his touch. "I'll be here for you. Whatever you need."

My head drops to his. "I'm lucky to have you."

"No, baby, it's me who's a lucky bastard."

With his kiss, my tense shoulders lower.

"I need to help Dori. Help her make arrangements," I struggle to say. "I'm not sure I'll make it to the fight tonight."

"It's all right if you can't. Either way, I'm teaching those fuckers a lesson."

"I want to be there." A single tear trickles down my cheek. "I want to see them suffer the way they made her suffer."

CHAPTER TWENTY-FOUR

DOMINIC

THE CLUBHOUSE IS BUZZING with life tonight. Every member and their ol' lady came out for the cage fight. No other MC members are allowed on a night like this. It's in-house and exclusive. Keeps the outcome private and the bruised egos of the losers contained. I plan on bruising more than their egos. I want them carried out on a fucking stretcher.

These men aren't my brothers. They don't know loyalty, honor, or respect the patch and the brotherhood it stands for. They're weak men. Men who get off on torturing and raping a woman who couldn't defend herself against them. I don't see them as equals. I'll never see them as equals.

Through the church room is another set of double doors. This is where we have our fight cage and private bar. Wooden benches line two walls, the cage taking up the other two. Between the benches and the fight cage are high top and low top tables with bar stools and chairs. Every seat is filled and the liquor is pouring heavily. A few bucks make their rounds on who's going to win the fight. It's fun play for my brothers, but for me, tonight is about so much more.

Lighting dim, it makes the blood stains on the cage mat harder to see, but it's there as a lingering memory of previous fights. Fights I've been a part of. Blood I've contributed myself. You don't last in the Serpents as long as I have without shedding some.

Across the cage, between the bars, I can see Drake and Levi getting themselves worked up for the fight. A slap to the face, some words for courage, a shot glass thrown back. Next to me are Mercy, John, Tex and RJ, some of my closest brothers. Mercy slaps my bare back and hands me a shot.

"Fuck 'em up."

With the shot thrown back, I bob my head. Shirt in my hands, I pull it over my head and toss it on a chair. Reaching into my pocket, I retrieve the brass knuckles I brought. That's an advantage with the cage fights—there are no rules.

Christian opens the cage door and dips his head, indicating Drake and Levi need to enter. Shirts off and in their jeans, they go into the cage, bouncing on the tips of their feet. They're wired and ready, probably high on coke too. Another advantage for me. With intent steps, I flex my muscles and give Christian a hard stare as I enter the cage.

The door locks behind us and I measure my opponents. Levi is tall and gangly, has speed, but will easily be put off balance. Drake has muscles, a solid core, slightly shorter than I am, but he always steps before he punches. It's been engrained in me to study the way every man I know fights, especially the ones closest to you.

Bloodshot eyes and their hyper energy are telltale signs they're high. The corner of my mouth raises when the circling starts. They'll come at me together at first, in hopes to overpower me, wear me down. Then once I'm tired, they'll split up and go for individual attacks to give themselves breaks and ensure I remain exhausted. They're dumb fucks if they think the fight will last that long.

They both charge and I slam into Levi. Hand to his throat, I ram him into the cage bars, knocking the wind out of him. Grip tight on his throat, I bring the brass knuckles down on his face. Blood spurts from his nose, then again from his busted lips.

"Fuuuck!" the word roars from my chest.

The cold steal slices across the lower left side of my back. Enraged, I turn on Drake and see him holding the bloody switchblade.

If blood is what they want, blood is what I'll give them.

Fast hand to his wrist, I wrap my elbow around his arm and kick his leg out from under him. The blade drops and I flip him over slamming him to the ground.

No hesitation, I snatch the blade and whip it across his cheek. Blood pours from the thin, neat cut. Flicking the blade into my other hand, I nail it into his thigh.

With the painkiller effects of the coke running through his system, he bellows from the wound, but still has a lot of fight. Seeing Levi come at me with a set of spiked knuckles, I get one brass-knuckled punch to Drake's face before I duck and roll, dodging the swing of Levi's arm.

Quick on my feet, I feel the warmth of my own blood running down my skin on the inside of my jeans. That's gonna need stitches. I need to move fast before I lose too much blood. Drake pulls the blade from his thigh and limps to his feet, holding the bars of the cage.

Circling one another, the crowd is alive with energy, screaming and hollering inaudible words at us. They're hungry for more.

Waving my fingers, I encourage their attack. Levi's got good legs, so he comes at me first. With an uppercut of the brass knuckles, he lands on his back. One hard boot to his face and he's lights out.

Drake circles me, blade in hand. With a fast swing, he grazes my arm, slicing it enough to make me bleed, but not enough to make me give a fuck. The fresh scent of copper fills my nostrils. Crimson red covers Drake's face and stains his jeans. Watching his feet, he lunges again, and I grab his hand, lock onto it, turn inside his arm and elbow his face, breaking his nose. Pulling his hand backward, the blade drops. With one swift turn, I put brass to bone, knocking him on his ass.

I only stop when I see his eyelids. He's out cold, and I heave a breath, controlling my fury before I murder him here in front of everyone. Rising to my feet, I pull the brass knuckles from my bloodied hand. The cage door opens for me, and I step out to hoots, hollers, pats on the back, and shots shoved into my hands. I down two for the pain.

All the faces are an adrenaline pumping blur until I see her—my Sparrow. Running to me, I enfold her in my arms, kissing her hard and fierce.

"I need to be inside you, baby."

"Take me now. I don't care."

"Fuck, I love you."

When her hand pulls back, she sees the blood and her eyes go wide.

"Dom, you're bleeding bad."

Raising my arm, she examines the cut. Mercy is beside us. He takes a look.

"C'mon, Dom, we need to get this stitched up."

With Erika under my arm, we follow Mercy out into the bar and restaurant area.

"Meet me in the bathroom. I'll get the kit and a bottle of Jack from under the bar."

With worried eyes, Erika looks up at me, and I wink at her.

"I'm fine, baby. Mercy knows how to do a quick stitch. How long you been here?"

Pushing open the bathroom door, I take a look at the damage in the mirror. The cut is easily four maybe five inches and it's bled too much already. Erika touches the outside of it, biting her lip in worry.

"Since you stabbed Drake in the thigh. He cut you deep. Should we go to the hospital?"

"Nah, baby, some hard liquor and your pussy will do the trick."

Her eyes light up and a glimpse of a smile tilts her lips.

Mercy walks in with the stitch kit and nods for me to assume the position. Tossing me the bottle, I twist the cap off and chug several swigs. Handing the bottle to Erika, she takes a couple herself, and my lips curve.

"You gonna watch?"

"Yes, I'm not leaving your side."

Mercy chuckles. "You ain't queasy about blood, are ya?"

"She's not," I answer for her when I see the shadow of Alee's memory cross her face.

"Good."

I grimace at the sting of the alcohol being poured over the wound and brace my hands on the porcelain sink. Wound cleaned, he pats it dry and takes a moment to prep the tools. By the time the first suture breaks through my skin, the alcohol has created a numbing effect.

Twenty minutes later, I stand and stretch from the

uncomfortable position I've been in. Erika examines the stitched cut.

"Obviously you've done this a few times before. It looks good."

Taking Erika in my arms, my hands snake up her shirt.

"Don't fuck up my handy work," Mercy laughs.

"I'm not promising anything," I quip.

Shaking his head and chuckling, he heads out. "See ya out there, brother. You done damn good teaching those shits what it is to be a Serpent."

With a nod, I appreciate his comment.

Thumbing over the nick on my arm, Erika looks at me with concern.

"I don't like seeing you cut up like this."

Putting my head to hers, I thumb her pouty lip.

"Did you see the other two?"

"I did. They deserved everything they got. I don't feel sorry for them."

Handing her the bottle of Jack, I encourage her to drink more.

"Have some more. You need it."

Snatching the bottle, she takes a couple swallows and grimaces at the bite.

"Dori's having her cremated. She's not even doing a service. I fought with her about it. How can she care so little?"

Another swallow of Jack and a single tear runs down her cheek.

"Your mother loves her, but her way of dealing is by not dealing."

"I want to go back out there. I want to drink, fuck, and forget."

Taking her face in my hand, I caress her cheek. "Only tonight," I tell her, wiping the tear away.

"Thank you," she replies, putting her head to mine. "But I'm not fucking in here," she adds playfully. "This bathroom reeks."

Squeezing her ass, I nudge her toward the door. "Get your ass out there then. I need to get you good and liquored up, so we can move onto the fucking."

"I'm thinking both holes tonight," she teases.

An aroused growl slips from my lips. "It's a done deal, baby. There's no taking that back."

My mouth crashes to hers as we exit the bathroom.

CHAPTER TWENTY-FIVE

ERIKA

Sitting in Dom's lap, the party has moved out to the bar and restaurant part of the clubhouse where the liquor is more easily accessible. With Drake and Levi needing to be hauled out of the cage, arms around shoulders of two Serpents on each side, that party room became a downer.

It took them a while to come to, and after they did, I'm pretty sure their asses were taken home or to the hospital. They're gone, I don't feel sorry, and the party is still raging on.

Warm from the liquor, and his touch, I suck my bottom lip and release it as Dom's hand moves over my breast, massaging it. Wiggling my ass over his jeans, I feel him thicken beneath me.

"You want my cock, don't you, baby?" he whispers before sucking my lobe into his mouth.

"Yes."

Reaching into my jeans, he circles his finger over my clit. Wet with need, he easily dips into my opening. Finger fucking me, he adds another digit, and I move back and forth over his erection, wanting more.

Lips moving like his fingers, he passionately licks and sucks my neck and ear. Turning my face to his, he dominates my mouth. Tongue to tongue, I match his pace, moaning into his lips as his fingers tease my building orgasm.

"Let's get a room. There's a couple down the hall."

Pulling his hand from my jeans, I whimper, and he winks with a grin. Guiding me through the room, we turn down the hall and pass the first room we hear noises from. Relieved that room is occupied, I follow him as he takes us farther down the hall to the next one. Opening the door, we find it empty, and Dom flicks on the light. The room looks like an actual room with a day bed and dresser in it.

When the door closes, Dom puts my back to it, one arm next to me as his other hand caresses my waist, pulling at my jeans as his lips steal my breath with his kiss. Clothes, there's too many of them. Shedding my jacket, I drop it on the floor. Hands to my shirt, he raises it off.

Cupping my breasts, he kisses the cleavage of both before pulling the fabric back and sucking each nipple into his mouth. Writhing against the door, I moan for him.

"Tell me how much you want my cock."

"Fuck, Dom, I need it. I need you inside me."

"I wanna feel your mouth around it first."

Backing him to the bed, I shove him on it, and he lands with his arms behind his head and a lascivious smirk on his sexy face.

Unbuttoning his jeans, I fold them down, and he raises his hips, so I can easily slide his jeans and briefs lower. His erection springs free, and his hand reaches for my face, caressing it as I take his cock in my hand. Hand moving to my hair, he lets out a breath of satisfaction as I fill my mouth with several inches of him.

"That's it, baby. Show me how much you want it."

Up and down, I suck and lick, taking him to the back of my throat and down it, then repeat it over and again.

"Fuuuuck, you make me wanna cum in your mouth."

Releasing him, I slide back and stand, slowly removing my jeans over my hips.

"No, babe, I want it in my pussy."

Coming to the edge of the bed, alluring green eyes watch me intently as I strip for him.

"You're beautiful, Sparrow. So fucking beautiful. Come're."

Rising, his hands take my bare hips and back me to the bed with him. Lips to mine, he moves me onto the bed, kissing me deep as he lays above me.

Fingers intertwined, he raises my hands over my head, claiming my mouth as he slides into me. Legs wrapped around him, the pleasure he brings with just one thrust ripples through my body. Drifting into euphoria, I move my hips to his tempo, losing myself to the incredible pleasure he gives.

The heat between us is palpable, our need for one another carnal. With each thrust, he takes me deeper into oblivion, satisfying my every desire.

Pulling out of me, I wonder the cause until his head brushes against my ass. Pushing forward, I expect the painful pressure, but he slides in easily, the action surprising him too by the look on his face.

Muscles relaxed, he moves in and out without causing me pain, the motion quickly becoming satisfying pleasure.

"Damn, your ass feels good. You like me fucking you like this?"

His lips feather mine as my orgasm builds.

"You feel amazing."

"I'm gonna take you harder. I wanna cum in your ass."

Releasing my arms, he raises up on his palms, then puts one hand under my leg and brings my knee toward my chest. Each time his cock thrusts forward, the pleasure pulses through my body. Our moans mingle as he takes me harder. Crying out, he gives my body its needed release. Head falling back, he slows his momentum, his cock thickening.

Letting go of my leg, he lays above me, gazing into my eyes.

"There's nothing better than being inside you."

With his kiss, I feel the passion, the love, the undeniable bond between us.

RETURNING TO THE PARTY, his arm drapes over my shoulder as I ask the bartender for two cups of water. Taking a seat on the barstool, he puts me between his legs, fussing with the ends of my hair as he watches me and the crowd around us.

"Hey brother, I thought you left."

I recognize Christian's voice behind me and go stiff. Dominic caresses my back in an attempt to soothe me.

"Nah, still here. We wanted some time alone to fuck."

With his wink to me, I laugh, taking the cup of water set on the bar. I don't turn around. I have no interest in acknowledging Christian which I know is disrespectful, but I don't care. Dom told me he voted against him on stripping Drake and Levi of their colors. I'd already lost my respect for Christian. That only made it worse.

"Drake and Levi were taken to the hospital. You really need to rough 'em up that bad?"

Dominic takes a sip from the solo cup, then sets it down, his gaze hardened.

"Alee's dead," he tells Christian, his tone cold. "She OD'd. It wasn't an accident."

"Fuck, man, when that happen?"

"This morning."

"Shit."

"I told ya, you didn't see what they did to her. I did. They got off easy. I let them live. Can't say I'll do the same for Ditch."

Pulling me to him, he kisses my head as I push back my tears.

"C'mon, baby."

"Dom," Christian calls.

"Another time, brother. I'm taken care of my girl tonight."

Ahead of us is a pool table and a round bar table next to it. Surrounding both are Dominic's friends. He hollers to them as we approach. A blond bombshell looks our way. She's tall with lengthy, silk, straight hair, ruby red lips and a black skin-tight dress showing off her long legs. Her pretty blue gaze sweeps over Dominic's bare chest under his jacket before measuring me up.

"Lookin' good, Dom. That was one hell of a fight."

"Save it, Roxy. I'm not in the fucking mood."

Leaning against the pool table, he places me between his legs and slips his tongue into my mouth, fisting my hair in his hand and squeezes my ass, putting me right up against his cock.

The blonde, Roxy, pounds her heels on the floor as she walks off. Dominic glances her direction and laughs to himself.

"Makin' a statement?" I ask, smiling at him.

"Yeah, you're my woman and she'll never be."

"I like that statement."

"Knew you would."

"Hey bro, how ya feelin'?" Mercy asks, patting him on the back, holding out a pool cue for him to take.

Accepting it, Dominic flashes a smile. "Still upright and breathing. What's the bet?" he asks, turning to see the action on the table.

"Just started. Eight-ball race. Five games. Twenty bucks a game."

Dom looks to me. "You play?"

Grinning, I nod. "I do."

Pocketing the three, four, then five balls, I hear a few mumbles and chuckles behind me.

"And she looks damn good doing it too," I hear Dom say.

Missing the six ball, I shrug and tip my head to John for his play.

"What'd I miss," I ask, returning to Dom and Mercy.

"We're talkin' about how you're sharking my money," Mercy laughs.

Lifting my drink to my lips, I take a sip. "I spent an entire summer at a pool hall across town. I learned a lot."

"I'm impressed and it's funny shit watching you rob my brothers' of their money." A smirk passes over his lips. Leaning in, his warm breath caresses my skin.

Hand on my hip, he tugs me to him. "Every time you bend over that table I think about how good it'll feel to have my cock in your ass again."

Glossy eyes flash a lecherous gaze at me.

Hand to his jeans, I rub his dick in front of whoever's looking.

"Keep thinking about it. I want it as much as you do."

Thumbing my lip, he lets it slowly slide from his finger.

"It's time we head out. I want you naked and spread in our bed."

CHAPTER TWENTY-SIX

ERIKA

What the hell did I do last night? Every muscle burns with each movement I make. Turning toward Dominic's heavy breathing, I grumble. It's his fault. All his fault. Fabric ties, cuffs, vibrator, sex toys; they're haphazardly strewn across the floor. Damn him and his erotically enticing ways.

"I hate you," I jest.

"No, you don't," he half grumbles, half laughs at me. You love me *and* all the shit we did last night."

"My body hates you," I reply playfully as I lay across his chest.

His muscled arm drapes over me, holding me against him. "With the way you were begging me to fuck you harder, I think your body loves what I do to it."

"Damn you, it does. I'm addicted to your love."

Arm tucked behind his head, he places his other hand on my neck and brings me to his lips.

"I like it that way."

Grumbling, I nuzzle into his chest. "My head," I whine.

"You need a beer and breakfast."

"Ugh, don't even mention alcohol."

Laughter rumbles from his chest.

"Let's get a shower, then I'll help you make breakfast."

"Will you carry me to the shower?"

"Only if you let me fuck you in the shower," he quips.

Dragging my body off him, I make a face at him. "You're insatiable."

With swift grace, he scoops me up in his arms. "I'm joking, baby. I'll give your pussy a break...for a few hours," he winks.

Setting me down just outside the shower, he turns the knobs to the desired temperature. As the water sets, he runs both hands over my hair, making a ponytail in his hand before tugging it back, lifting my gaze to his.

"Thank you for helping me forget last night."

"I'll help you forget every night for as long as you need me to."

Testing the water temp, he seems satisfied. With a hand, he helps me step into the shower. As I rinse under the warm water, he gathers shampoo in his hands.

I go to reach for the shampoo and he stops me. Putting his hands in my hair, he lathers the soap in. Eyes closed, I enjoy the soothing massage of his fingers.

Tears of appreciation gather in my eyes. "I don't know what I'd do without you right now. I'd be lost, broken."

Running my locks through his fist, he wrings out the soap and water.

"You would've found a way to get through it."

The reality of Amberlee' s death stabs at me, and my chest constricts, fighting back tears.

"How do you know that?"

He quietly laughs to himself. "You're like me."

The touch of the warm washcloth on my body keeps the tears at bay. I focus on his intense green eyes as he reaches lower, the washcloth caressing my skin. Between my legs, he lingers, moving the cloth forward and back in a delicate motion. Hand to my jaw, his thumb grazes my cheek, wiping away a stray tear before his masculine lips cover mine.

Withdrawing his hand, he puts his arms around me as I lay against his chest, letting the warm water soothe away the soreness in my muscles.

"I love you."

His chin rests on my head, his hands moving over my back, rubbing me.

PLACING ham on the second plate, I smile at him as he takes the plates and carries them into the dining room. The toast pops, and I slather them with butter before joining him. As usual, he's put an empty chair close to his. I love that he does that. He always wants me within arm's reach, I adore that about him. As masculine as he is around other men, he's far more affectionate than I ever expected him to be.

"Last night...you were amazing the way you fought against them. I wish Alee could've seen them suffer."

Taking a bite, I notice his brows pinch inward.

"For a while, I want you with me. You can join me while I take care of some business, then we'll go to the range."

"You're worried about them retaliating?"

"Not worried." Lifting his glass, he takes a drink. "Prepared. I know how men like them think." His thoughts have darkened. I can see it in his detached expression and icy stare.

"What business?"

"I need to stop by some properties, collect rent, check on some things."

In an effort to pull him from his thoughts, I pick up his empty plate and kiss him on the cheek.

"That was good. Thank you."

After dropping the dishes in the sink to be cleaned later, we get our jackets and boots.

On the back of his Harley, I enjoy the feel of the wind whipping over my face and his warm strong body in front of me. The ride is peaceful, a needed distraction. I worry how long it'll take until I don't need distractions. In an effort to not think about Amberlee, she becomes the very focus of my mind. The image of her pretty red hair, golden hazel eyes, and tilted, cocky smirk has tears welling in my eyes, my throat dry, my chest tightening. The most painful part is the fear I'll lose the detailed memory of her beautiful face. It's difficult to accept I'll never get to hear her playful laugh or have her stroke my hair. She should be here. I'd give anything to see her one more time.

She was so young, so full of life, and now she's gone while the men who hurt her are free to do what they want. I imagine the fight will cause conflict in the Serpents. Dominic's grudge will never be laid to rest. How can Christian expect him to let it go, to have us ride alongside them?

When the bike slows, I look at the gray two-story house where we've stopped. Dominic parks the bike and steps off. Attention on me, his head tilts, expression empathetic.

"You thinkin' about Alee?"

"Yeah, I couldn't help it," I wipe a couple stray tears. "I miss her."

"Ah, baby," Taking my hand, he helps me off the bike, taking me in his arms. "I know you do. I'll get through these stops as quick as I can, then get you home."

Letting go, he kisses me.

"Stay with the bike."

Sexy in his jeans and jacket, I watch him take the three steps onto the porch and knock on the door. A man answers. His gaze sweeps the horizon before he hands Dominic a wad of cash. With a nod, he says a few words, then the man closes the door. Returning to the bike, Dominic puts the cash into a secure spot in his saddle bag.

"A few more of these stops and we'll be done."

"What's the cash for?"

Dominic makes a sound against his cheek. "This is the kind of thing I wanna keep you away from. Can you be ok with that?"

It's difficult not knowing the activity he's involved in, but a stop like this, cash like that, leaves only a few possibilities; drugs, protection, a payoff, or the guy's buying something from the Serpents.

"Yeah, just be careful."

"I guess I got to," Gripping the bars, he climbs on, "now that you've given me a reason to."

Looking at me, he watches me climb on behind him. "Ready?"

Arms around him, I rub my thumb over his abs through his shirt.

"I am."

Five more stops like the first and Dominic brings me to the clubhouse. Pulling a smaller black leather bag from the inside of his saddlebag, it hangs from his arm as he puts the other around me.

Inside the clubhouse, there are a few bikers. Some are Serpents, some aren't. Cinderville has always been a pass-through for bikers. I wouldn't be surprised if the ones in here today aren't from around here. I've never seen their emblems, so I'd say that's the case. Two men are putting down burgers and beers. On their black jackets are a silver skull and crown. Their patch says, Kings. Dominic's attention is instantly drawn to them, one of the men in particular.

"Jake fucking Castle."

An attractive man with dark hair, vivid brown eyes, and beastly arms almost as big as Dominic's turns his head our direction. Standing from the chair, he and Dominic give one another a brotherly hug and pat each other's back.

"Damn, Dom. It's been a while."

"Years, man, it's been years. How long you in town?"

"Only tonight. We head out tomorrow."

"What brings you back here?"

"Business, we needed specialty parts and an excuse for a ride." He pats his friend's shoulder. "This is my brother, Nix."

Nix stands, taller than Dominic and Jake, with gorgeous green eyes and black medium length hair. With a curve of his lips, he gives us a friendly smile.

"Jake was telling me earlier how y'all used to run together as boys. It's good to meet ya, brother."

"You too, man." Dominic points at Jake's jacket. "So you're a Kings. Not surprised to see you in leathers. Knew it would happen."

One hand in his jeans pocket, Jake shrugs. "It was a

long road to the Kings, but I'm where I belong now. How about you? Like father, like son."

"Sometimes too much." They both chuckle at something the two of them know, clearly about Dominic's father.

Putting an arm around me, he makes me the center of attention.

"This is my girl, Erika."

Looking me over, they both give a gesture of approval.

"Good to meet you. I'm Dominic's cousin," Jake tells me.

Now the familiarity between them makes sense. I can even see a bit of a resemblance too, except for their eyes. Standing between the three of these men, I feel intimidated. Each one of them is as hot as the next. Together, they're a woman's fantasy.

Handing me the black bag, Dominic nods toward Christian's office. "Baby, can you take this to him?"

"Yeah." I take the bag from his outstretched hand and glance back at them as Dominic joins their table and gets absorbed into their conversation.

Knocking first, I enter Christian's office to find him sending a text. He raises his head and seems surprised to see me. Immediately, his eyes go to the black bag. He pulls out a drawer at his desk.

"Drop it in here. Where's Dom?"

"Out there. His cousin Jake is passing through town."

Christian closes the drawer, a grin on his face. "No shit."

"Yeah, they're out there eating and talking."

Christian quickly stands from his desk.

"You know him too?"

"Yeah, Jake lived here when we were kids before him and his mom moved to Georgia."

Christian seems eager to see him. He closes the door behind us and we walk down the hall in silence. In the clubhouse, there's boisterous laughter from their table.

"You're a father?" Dominic asks Jake.

"Hard to believe, right?" Nix jokes. "Liz has had him wrapped around her finger since the moment he met her."

"Shit, I know the feeling. Been that way with Erika."

My presence catches his attention. His sexy smile widens and he pulls me onto his lap.

As soon as Jake sees Christian, he stands, and they go through their own greeting.

Hand on my hip, Dominic caresses my bare skin, relaxing me with the simplest touch.

"Where y'all stayin' tonight?"

"We'll find a hotel somewhere around here."

"Nah, brother, you both can stay with me." Dominic looks to me. "Can you cook us something good?"

Pleased he asked, a smile briefly lifts the corners of my mouth. "Of course."

"Well, hell, I'm not gonna turn down a free bed and a hot meal. Thanks, man."

ALL THREE OF them are settled around the table talking about bikes, riding, and memories of when they were young. I've learned Jake is with Nix's sister, Liz and they just had a baby boy which Jake is thrilled about. With the way he talks about Liz, I can tell how much he loves her and his son.

With a sideways glance, Dominic checks on me. Excusing himself, he enters the kitchen and fills the space behind me, putting his warm arms around my waist.

"Smells good. Thanks for doing this." He places a soft kiss against my neck.

"I'm happy to. Your cousin and Nix are nice guys."

"They really are good men. I haven't seen Jake in years. It's good to catch up."

I point to the cabinet. "Can you grab some plates?"

"Yeah, baby. Anything else you need?"

"Just a fresh beer," I jingle the empty bottle in my hand, "I'm out."

After getting the plates out of the cupboard, he brings me a beer while I put food on the plates. He helps me carry them in, and I join the guys, ready to eat.

"It's crazy seeing Christian as the President of the Serpents," Jake tells Dominic.

Lowering his beer from his lips, Dominic's expression turns serious.

"I wanna say he's not the boy you remember, but these days something's changed. His focus for the Serpents isn't what it used to be. Even as outlaws, we always had a code. Now he chooses to keep members who don't respect the patch because he needs the numbers against our rivals."

"The Serpents still deal in heavy business?"

Dominic takes another drink of his beer. I can see he's thinking something over.

"Serpent business is Serpent business," he smirks at Jake.

Chuckling, Jake fills his fork with more food. "Always loyal."

"Nothing's changed there. How's your mom? She still in Georgia?"

A frown pulls at Jake's lips. "She died a few years ago. Overdose," Jake explains.

My fork drops, and Dominic reaches for me, rubbing my arm as the pain slams into my chest. Nix and Jake's attention whip to me, reading my expression.

"You all right?" Nix asks, concerned.

"Her sister just died, overdose," Dominic shares.

"Shit, I'm sorry Erika. I know how hard it is," Jake replies, his tone rich with empathy.

Biting my lip, I refuse to let the tears fall. I take a breath, and Dominic slides my chair closer, rubbing my back. For a few minutes, everyone eats in silence. I feel bad for bringing down the mood.

"I'm sorry."

"Nothing to apologize for," Nix assures me. "We all understand the pain of losing someone. What was your sister's name?"

"Amberlee. She was beautiful, bold red hair and a sassy personality."

"Nix would've liked her." Jake nudges Nix. "He's got a thing for redheads."

Nix rolls his eyes. Their jesting makes me laugh.

"Does the pain ever go away?" I ask suddenly, feeling a little foolish that it slipped out.

"No," Jake says with feeling. "It'll always hurt when you think of her, but the daily pain does go away."

With his hand around my neck and shoulder, Dominic pulls me to him, kissing my head, soothing me with his affection.

"It's too bad y'all have to leave. I like you a hell of a lot better than some of the Serpents."

As he chews, Dominic smiles. It's wonderful to see him so comfortable and happy around these fellow riders.

"If you two ever want to visit Nashville, my door's always open," Jake tells us.

"I'd love to," I admit, my gaze glancing from Jake to Dominic and back.

Jake tips his head at Dominic. "Now you got an excuse for a ride."

"We'll take a trip," he assures me.

PUTTING BACK BEERS, their laughter echoes into the kitchen. I finish the dishes and join them in the living room. Feeling tired, I snuggle up to Dominic on the couch. Laying my head on his shoulder, he kisses it.

"Baby, you look exhausted."

"I am."

"Go on up. I'll hang here a while, then join you."

"Ok, love you."

Kissing him, he holds me to him, giving me a passion-filled kiss in return, stirring my arousal.

"Thanks for dinner."

"You're welcome."

"Yeah, that chicken was great," Nix says, lowering his beer. "We appreciate you cookin'."

"Nice meeting you," Jake says with a tip of his head and his beer.

"You too." And I mean it.

As I ascend the stairs, I can hear them still.

"That's a nice woman you got there. Don't fuck it up."

"He knows what he's talking about. He almost fucked things up with Liz a couple of times."

"He'll never let me live it down," Jake quips.

Dominic expresses amusement with a short laugh.

"No need to worry, brother. She's it. She's the one I want with me on this crazy ass ride of life."

The usual stair creaks beneath me and my beaming smile widens as I take the last couple steps and turn down the hall to our room.

ROLLING OVER, Dominic runs his hand over my hip and side as he presses his erection into my ass. Lips sucking my ear lobe into his mouth, I moan when the tips of his fingers press against my clit.

I don't know what time it is, but it feels early. Not that I care when his cock head is against my ass, turning me on.

"I want you to ride me, baby."

"Ass or pussy?"

The hair on my skin rises when his hot breath and sexy voice rumbles against my ear.

"Both."

Lying on his back, he runs his hands over my body as I straddle him. One hand plays with my nipple, pinching it to a pointed peak as his other slips between my cheeks, fingering my tight hole.

Stretching my arm out to the nightstand, I gather lubricant and place some in my hand. Fisting his erection, I pump up and down, and his eyelids lower, his hips rising slightly, matching my strokes.

His fingering gets rougher, stretching and opening me for him, making me wet with need. My strokes stop, and I hold his cock in my hand as I raise up on my knees, putting his head to my ass. A pleasured sound draws from his lips as I slowly slide onto him. Laying forward on his chest, he holds my ass cheeks as he thrusts up, pounding into me.

"Shit, baby."

"You feel good too, so good."

His lips take mine, loving me with his mouth as his cock fucks my ass, giving me the pleasure I desired. Gripping me, he pulls out and flips us, putting me on my back. Hands under my knees, he brings them toward my chest and holds them down as he thrusts into my pussy. Taking me hard, I bite my lip, trying to be quiet.

"I don't care if they hear."

Releasing my legs, he sits back on his. Straddling my legs around him, I'm still on my back. Entering my pussy, he tugs me tighter against him. A loud groan escapes my lips as he pinches my clit and thrusts into me. Rising on his knees, he lifts me off my ass. Hands on my legs, he holds me up as he fucks me. I'm completely in his control at this angle and I love it. Fast and hard thrusts draw more cries of pleasure from my mouth.

"Oh God, Dom,"

"That's it, baby. Come for me."

I do and come hard, soaking his cock. I ride the high as he thrust several more times before he reaches his orgasm.

Letting my legs down, I know I have a sated grin on my face. He lowers on top of me, kissing me.

"I love how much I turn you on."

"I do too. You seem to have an endless supply of positions and toys. It'll never get boring."

"Hell no, it'll never get boring. Not with how much kink we both like."

Enclosing my breast in his hand, he sucks at my nipple, and I giggle at his playful nibbling.

"Hearing you say that, sounds like you're thinking about us in the future."

"I heard you just before I reached the top of the stairs. You're it for me too, Dom. My forever."

Wet lips leave a trail of kisses from my breasts to my neck. "Forever, huh? You willing to have clipped wings?"

I laugh as his lips nip at my neck. "What do you mean?"

"You're my Sparrow, forever mine, forever having clipped wings."

Kissing him, I hold his face to mine, looking into his sensuous emerald eyes.

"You're a fool if you think my wings would be clipped. With you, I'm forever free."

CHAPTER TWENTY-SEVEN

ERIKA

THE WEEK HAS GONE BY TOO FAST. I'm not ready to join my mother in collecting Amberlee's ashes. Holding the urn makes it real, makes her truly gone, and I've been refusing to accept it. There are moments I've had where I've daydreamed of going over to Dori's and seeing Amberlee there, putting her makeup on, curling her hair, getting ready to go out for the night. I remember the day she did my hair and makeup for Dominic. She wasn't always great at expressing her affection verbally, but she had her ways of showing how much she cared like she did that day.

Dominic thinks I would've gotten through her loss without him. He has more confidence in me than I do. Each day, his love and affection has snuffed out the pain. If not for him, I'd still be living in the house she was attacked in. I know I would've been taken and raped too. It's something we haven't spoken about, but I know he's aware of it, just as I am. By moving me in with him, he saved my life.

Sitting next to him on the couch, I put on my heels while watching him put his gun back together after being cleaned.

"I want to come with you," I insist.

"No." His attention doesn't leave the gun. "I told you, this is the exact kind of business I don't want you involved in."

"Is it illegal?"

He doesn't reply. Shoulders tense, he puts the magazine in and thumbs the safety switch. Putting it in his overnight bag, he zips it closed.

"I don't like this," I admit. I can hear the worry etched in my own voice.

Christian has him prepping for an out-of-state run. It's the first time Dominic is leaving me alone. Admittedly, I'm nervous about it, but he tried to soothe those fears by taking me to the range for shooting practice. He doesn't like the trip either and we already got into one heated discussion about me joining him. He was adamant I can't come. That's how I know it's likely something illegal.

I don't want him to go and that's been hard on him. I sense he feels torn between his duties with the Serpents and staying with me. His duties are also keeping him from being with me today when I pick up Amberlee's ashes and he doesn't like that either.

Sitting back against the couch, he rubs his forehead. The stress is written on his face.

"Are you mad at me that I keep pushing the issue?"

"It's irritating me, but no I'm not mad at you. I know today will be rough for you and I can't be there for you. That's bothering me."

Scooting closer, I lay my legs over his, and he sets his hand on my thigh and rubs it.

"I don't want to keep pushing the issue. I get I can't go. I'm just...having a hard time letting you go."

"I know, baby. I feel the same. This run is shitty timing, but it needs done, and I need to be there."

"You don't think you'll get held up, do you? I can handle you being back tomorrow night, but any longer and I'm going to get antsy."

"No, business will be in and out. We won't stick around."

"Mmm," I whine, laying my head on his shoulder.

His strong hand touches my face, caressing it before he lifts my chin to his gaze.

"I'm going to miss you, a lot. Keep the gun with you at all times. And be ready for me to pound the fuck out of your pussy when I get home."

Reaching between my legs, he slips his hand beneath my skirt and moves my underwear to the side. Circling my clit, I moan just before his lips lock to mine in a passionate display of need.

"Do we have time before you have to leave?" he asks, his tone seductive.

"I'll make time."

Laying me on my back, he glides my skirt up my thighs, exposing my black silk panties. My eyes lower from his lascivious green ones to the bulge in his jeans he sets free. Keeping my underwear held to the side, he slides between my legs, filling me, gratifying my insatiable desire for him.

DRIVING UP TO THE HOUSE, I sit in the driveway taking several slow, calming breaths. Placing my hand on the door handle of the Camaro, I stiffen. My hand drops and instead I reach for my cell phone to text Dominic.

I can't do this.

Yes, you can. Don't go in the house. Have Dori come out. I'm sorry I can't be there.

Dori walking in front of the vehicle pulls my thoughts back to the present.

It's ok. Be careful. I love you.

She opens the passenger door and gets in, the door closing loudly. "Figured you didn't want to come in," she says casually, not looking at me.

"It's hard. I don't want to accept that she's not in there. Picking up her ashes makes it real."

"Try walking in there every day." There's sorrow in her voice.

"I don't know how you do it."

"I'm moving out. I can't keep doing it."

Surprised, I stare over at her long, jet black hair and the face I look nothing like.

"When?"

"I need to finish packing tonight and tomorrow. I want to be gone by the end of this weekend."

"You need help packing?"

Dori's attention is finally drawn to me. Rather than the bloodshot eyes I'm used to seeing, they're clear blue with tears welling up in them.

"You'd be willing to do that?"

"Yes. I don't want you staying here either."

Her head drops, a tear rolls down her cheek.

"Do you hate me?"

Seeing the hurt, feeling it emanating from her, it tightens my throat and chest.

"No, I don't hate you."

Wiping her stray tears, she collects herself and looks out the window, her thoughts becoming distant.

"We should get going."

Putting the car in reverse, I back out and take the long, dreaded ride to the funeral home.

RUBBING my finger over the smooth exterior of the urn, I do my best to process that Amberlee's ashes are in there. Having her close to me like this gives me strange comfort. Sitting on her bed, I hold it tight against my chest and let the grieving tears flow.

Thinking of what she'd say to me, I close my eyes and imagine her stroking my hair. She'd tell me life is too short to spend it being sad. She'd tell me to live life to the fullest, no regrets. She'd tell me to cry for her today, then smile when I remember her every day after.

"I promise I will," I tell her.

Knot in my throat, I stand from her bed and let out a breath, wiping the tears from my cheeks. Carrying the urn to the living room, I leave it sitting on the shelf against the wall and gather an empty cardboard box. While Dori packs her room, I told her I'd pack up Amberlee's. Dori set aside what she wanted which was some clothes, jewelry, pictures, and a couple keepsake items that were special to Amberlee. She told me to take what I wanted out of the rest and anything after that was going to be donated or sold.

Looking through her closet, I laugh to myself at Amberlee's bold style. The majority of the clothes show more ass or boob than I'd like, but I still find a few pieces I'd like to have of hers. It'll be nice to think of her when I wear them. After placing them in the box, I sit on the bed to answer Dom's call.

"We're heading out soon. You doing ok?"

"Yeah, having her urn gave me more closure than I expected. Dori wants to move out. I'm at the house packing up Amberlee's things."

"Baby, I don't want you there. You should head home."

"I won't be long. Dori needs the help. She doesn't have anyone."

There's a pause and a long sigh.

"You got your gun with you?"

"Yeah, I brought it in with me."

"You got me worried now. I don't like you being there. Text or call as soon as you leave."

"I will. I want you to be careful too. I'm nervous about your trip."

"I know. Don't worry about me though. This is usual business for me."

"Ok."

"I love you. Remember to call or text. Don't stay long."

"Love you too."

Disconnecting is difficult. We're both just as worried about the other, and I don't need to give him added stress when he probably already has a lot going on, so I'll stay another hour, then help her pack more in the morning.

The sound of movement in the doorway draws my attention. Dori is standing there looking around Amberlee's room. Her blue eyes are red and puffy, her expression filled with sorrow.

"I'm gonna pick up a pizza for us. You hungry?"

"I am, but you don't have to pick it up. I can call for delivery."

"I need to get cigarettes too, so I'll pick up the pizza while out."

"All right," I say, frowning.

"Don't be long though. I can't stay late."

"Ok, I'll see ya in a bit."

Dori disappears out the door and I wonder if I'll see her again tonight or not. I'll put in the hour of packing and after that if she's still not back, she can eat alone whenever she does make it home.

I hear the front door close and get back to sorting through Amberlee's closet. It doesn't take me long to pick out a few things, so I move onto her drawers. Sitting on her nightstand is her phone. Picking it up, I turn it on.

The usual logo pops up and then her artsy screensaver appears. There are notifications, and I figure I might as well clear them and respond to any friends before calling the cell phone company and having it turned off.

There are several texts requesting drug deals which I ignore, then below, there's a text from Ditch. I notice she's already read it. Clicking on it, I see several pictures have been sent. As soon as I look at the photos, I drop the phone and bring my hand to my mouth as I inhale a horror-filled breath.

He was taunting her with pictures of her assault. Photos of her abuse that they'd taken while she was unconscious. No wonder she was being distant. Even after her assault, they were making her relive it again and again. The fucking bastards.

Rumbling of motorcycles in the distance startle me

to my feet. Pulling the curtain of her window back, I search outside. It's clear. No one out there. I take a breath of relief. Picking her phone up from the bed, I move the box aside. It's time to get the hell out of here. I'll help Dori first thing in the morning.

Crossing the living room, I gather my purse and head to the door. Opening it, I step out and several hands instantly take hold of me, shoving me back inside. The door slams behind them.

"Hi, bitch. We've been waiting for your fucking mother to leave."

Ditch and Drake tower over me, their expressions deadly. Backing up, I slowly reach inside my purse.

"No, you don't."

Drake draws a gun from his waistband and points it straight at my head. Fear seizes my body and I stop moving.

Tilting the gun toward my old room, he nods toward it. "Get in the fucking room."

I can see the danger in his eyes. With the cut and marks on his face from Dominic's brass knuckles, his scowl is even more terrifying. Glancing over their shoulders, I know they haven't locked the front door. I need to distract them, to get to the door. Throwing my purse to the left, I bolt right, leaping over the couch in an effort to get away.

I'm just within reach of the door when Ditch slams his body against it, locking it in place. A deafening boom goes off in the room and I cower at the sound.

Drake's given me a warning shot. The bullet is in the chair next to me.

Ditch is on me before I have time to think. Gripping my hair, he rips out some as he drags me to my feet.

"We're gonna have a lot of fun with you."

My cheek instantly burns from his backhanded slap. A whimper escapes my mouth and he laughs at me.

"You're a soft little bitch. Your sister could take a hell of a lot of pain without crying about it." He smirks at Drake, "It's not gonna take much to make her bleed."

With his head turned, I claw at his face, going for his eyes. Overpowering me, he slams me into the wall, knocking my breath out of me.

"I'm gonna enjoy hurting you, then I'm gonna enjoy fucking your cunt."

"You know Dom will kill you for this," I spit back.

He clicks his tongue against the inside of his cheek. "Dom can't find out we're the ones who beat and raped you, so we're gonna have to kill you when we're done. We'll make it look like the Jackals got a hold of you. Dom won't have any reason to come after us."

Trembling, my eyes widen.

"Aw look at that. The bitch thought we were going to let her live when we were done with her," he says to Drake.

"That's because she's a dumb bitch. Bring her in the room. Let's get her clothes off."

Kicking at Ditch, I fight with everything I have to

get out of his arms. Adrenaline pumps through me, giving me added strength. Ditch's grip on me loosens, but it's reinforced with Drake grabbing me.

Ditch pins my arms together and Drake grabs my legs, together they drag me into my old room, my heels falling off along the way. I'm thrown forcefully on the bed, my head knocking into the bed frame. It's not hard enough to be an issue but leaves me temporarily dizzy.

Hands come at me quickly, trying to force my clothes off. I'm not giving up. If they're going to kill me, then I have nothing to lose. My purse is still in the hallway. I just need to get to it. Scratching, clawing, swinging, and biting, I give it my all, trying to take out an eye or kick one of them in the nuts.

Shoved onto my belly, my face is forced into the pillow, and I struggle to breathe. One of them puts my hands together behind my back and I feel something being tied around them. Pulled tight, I recognize the sound of zip ties. Tears form in my eyes. Ditch is paying me back, tying me up like I did him.

I suck in a breath when I'm turned over. Backhanded, my cheek burns severely as tears descend down my cheek.

"Cut her shirt and bra off," Drake tells Ditch.

Knife pulled from his jeans, Ditch's tongue licks at his lip ring as he cuts into the front of my shirt, opening it wide and exposing my bra and chest.

"I'll give you credit, little sis. You got real nice tits. Bet Dom likes fucking them."

Bra pulled away from my skin, he slips the knife beneath it and with one quick forceful slice, the bra pops open.

"Sss, look at these," he says to Drake, reaching for my chest. Scrambling back, I avoid his touch.

Ringing suddenly goes off. Drake and Ditch stiffen.

"It's her phone."

Drake keeps an eye on me while Ditch disappears into the hallway. He returns with my purse. Pulling the phone from it, he looks worried.

"It's Dom."

"Doesn't matter. I told you he's on a gun run. Won't be back until tomorrow."

"Look what else she's got." Ditch pulls the gun from my purse and I swallow down the tight knot in my throat.

"She was gonna shoot us, Drake. I think we need to teach her a lesson about manners."

With a fast movement, Drake grabs my legs and drags me to the end of the bed. Forcing my skirt down my legs, he reaches for my underwear. I try to fight him and he slaps me hard across the face.

"Cut these off too," he orders Ditch.

My adrenaline is starting to falter. My body is getting tired and fear is doing strange things to my mind. I try to shimmy away from him and Drake raises his arm to hit me again. I turn my head away and stop squirming.

"Good girl, you learn quick."

His hand whips across my face and a cry breaks free. "But I still enjoy it."

The fabric of my underwear is cut and torn away, exposing me. Below, I'm completely bare and vulnerable. The hot sticky air on my naked flesh and their predatory gazes churn my stomach.

My torn shirt and bra are spread out on each side of me. Ditch quickly changes that by cutting the straps and tearing the rest of the fabric. Curling up, I try to get away. Drake fists my ankles, pulling my legs back down.

"No, bitch, we want to see it all."

My legs are spread and they look me over with disgusting grins.

"She's got a nice cunt, doesn't she?" Drake asks Ditch, his hands keeping my legs open.

"Yeah, quit wasting time looking. I'm ready to fuck it," his words are cold as he adjusts his dick in his jeans.

Tears pour down my cheeks. I don't know if I'll make it out of this, but I'm not ready to accept defeat. The belt on Drake's pants jingle and I take that opportunity to roll away. Laughter breaks out behind me. I'm pinned down by the weight of one of them, while I hear pants unzipping.

"Please don't," I beg.

"Crying and begging won't stop us, little sis. You owe us this."

Stroking his hand through my hair, Ditch makes a fist and pulls my head back.

"Ease up. I need to pull her back farther."

Ditch's weight lifts and I'm dragged down the bed.

"That's it. Turn her over."

Ditch rotates me, my shoulders aching. I can't see what's going on behind Ditch because his weight is on my stomach, his torso blocking my view of Drake. More tears stream down my cheeks as fear courses through my veins. I hear the sound of Drake licking something and Ditch stares down at me, his brown eyes evil as he laughs. Fingers penetrate me and I immediately scream.

Ditch swings his arm to hit me, then stops abruptly when he hears the pounding on the front door. They both freeze, looking at one another.

"Get the fucking door," Ditch tells Drake.

Drake grumbles and comes into view. Tucking his dick into his pants, he zips up his jeans.

Ditch raises Dominic's gun to my face, pushing the muzzle to my lips. "Ssh"

Raising my hips, I try to buck him off, and he snickers, "You're a feisty bitch."

The noise of the front door opens, followed by a piercing gunshot. Ditch and I both look toward the hall.

"Mom!" I scream.

Fear engulfs me. Between my tears, I fight under him. Heavy footsteps come down the hall and I'm terrified of Drake's return.

Ditch inhales a sharp breath and I glance up. Gun pointed at Ditch's chest, Dominic fires. Ditch falls backward off the bed, landing on the floor, blood pouring out of his open wound. One step forward, Dominic aims the gun again. Another boom echoes through the room. Ditch stops twitching, his body going slack.

Tucking the gun back into his waistband, Dominic turns to me, carefully helping me up. He turns me away from him and cuts the zip ties, freeing my arms. The ache in my shoulders ease, and I turn around, falling into his open arms, crying into his chest.

"I got you, baby. It's over. They're never gonna be able to hurt you again."

My tears are hard to control. Rubbing my back, he tries to calm me.

"Did they rape you?"

I shake my head and his tense shoulders drop.

"Look at me."

Raising my chin, he looks me in the eyes, his own filled with too many emotions to read.

"Are you able to look for clothes and drive home? I need to take care of this."

"I'll help you," I mutter.

"No, baby. I want your hands clean. I know who to call. I just need you safe at home. Wait for me there."

"What about Dori?"

"I'll handle it."

Glancing over my shoulder, Dominic pulls my attention back to him.

"Don't look. It's better you don't."

"Please," I beg. "Please be careful. I can't lose you."

"You won't. But you gotta get out of here, fast, baby. I don't have a lot of time."

"Ok."

Leaving him right now is a struggle, but I understand what needs done. Rushing to Amberlee's room, I grab a sweatshirt and a pair of shorts. I can hear Dominic talking on the phone in my room. I don't linger. I do as he asked and get out fast.

CHAPTER TWENTY-EIGHT

DOMINIC

IN THE PASTY YELLOW KITCHEN, I down another shot, waiting for Mercy to arrive. Different thoughts cross my mind. What if I hadn't decided to come back for her? They would've taken her from me. They would've beat her, raped her repeatedly, then they would've killed her and framed someone else, so I didn't come after them. No doubt that was their plan. It's the only plan that would keep them alive.

Shooting them wasn't difficult for me to do. I've killed men before, this was no different. It's the cleanup that's the problem. Getting rid of bodies is a messy job. A job that takes more than one man. I hate having to bring Mercy into this even though I know he'll understand.

As for Dori, it's a good thing she already planned on moving, because this house will need to go up in flames, burning away any evidence of what happened here.

When I hear the rumble of his Harley, I take another shot, then meet him at the door.

Inside, he closes and locks the door behind him. His gaze goes to Drake's body.

"Stupid fucks. Got what they deserved. She ok?"

"I don't know yet. She's home waiting for me. I didn't want her involved in this."

"I understand, brother. What about Dori?"

"She'll have to pack the important shit quick."

"Where is she?"

"Probably out selling herself for drugs. Christian cut her off. I left her a message to get her ass back here."

"All right. Let's get this shit handled."

ENTERING THE BACK DOOR, it's late. I expect her to be asleep, but she's holding a glass of liquor in between her hands, shaking on the couch. Stripping out of my filthy shirt, I toss it in the trash. Washing my arms and hands in the kitchen sink, I clean up some, enough I can at least hold her. Coming into the living room, her fear filled eyes meet mine.

"Dominic..."

She falls apart in front of me and I go to her. Sitting on the couch, I pull her into my lap.

"Ssh, baby, it's going to be ok. Everything is taken care of," I assure her, stroking her hair and face.

"You came back?"

"I changed my mind about taking you. It didn't feel right leaving you here. I was too damn worried, and if I couldn't stay and protect you, you were better off with me."

"Drake knew about the gun run. Knew you wouldn't be back until tomorrow. What if...what if this was planned? They were going to kill me and blame the Jackals. You would've gone after them. You would've taken them out. Taken out Christian's problem for him."

Sitting forward, I take her drink and empty it as the things she's said takes residence in my thoughts.

"They had to of started following me this morning. How did they know when to follow me? Where I'd be?"

My jaw tightens. Rage is a snake slithering up my spine. The only Serpents who knew about the gun run was Christian, John, Mercy, and me. We keep these runs on a need to know basis. The fewer people involved, the fewer chances of fuck ups or word slipping to the police. I know without a doubt in my mind Mercy and John didn't tell Drake about it.

Returning my attention to Erika, it's like a blade ripping through my chest seeing the fear and worry in her eyes.

"You think I'm right, don't you?"

Bringing her face close, I kiss her forehead. With her swollen tender cheeks and busted lip, I don't want to hurt her.

"Tomorrow we're packing up. I need to take care of some things, then we're leaving this town."

Shock steals her breath.

"Where are we going?"

"To Nashville."

"What about the Serpents? Can you leave them?"

"Don't worry about anything but packing the important things we need. If it's replaceable, don't pack it."

"What are you gonna do?"

Running my fingers through her freshly washed hair, I massage the base of her neck.

"What I do best."

CHAPTER TWENTY-NINE

DOMINIC

FIRST THING FIRST, making sure Dori got her shit out. It's two in the morning and everyone on this shitty side of town is either passed out from drugs or alcohol or still partying hard. You know you're in a shithole area when gunshots are fired and no one calls the police.

House vacant, I walk through each room, gasoline container in hand, pouring it over everything, including Christian's stash of drugs in the garage. Dropping the can by my feet, I retrieve the lighter from my pocket. With a flick of the flint wheel, a flame rises from the Zippo. Tossing it onto the floor, I watch the flames quickly ascend toward the ceiling.

Stripping my Serpent jacket, I fist it in my hand, pain burning my insides. With a difficult breath, I toss it into the flames. Grabbing the can, I leave behind the burning house.

LOOKING DOWN at my cell phone in my hand, my jaw hardens as I read the messages from Christian. He's pissed I bailed on the gun run and wants to know what the hell is going on. Mercy is doing damage control for me. He caught up with them and is giving me a cover—my bike is broken down and I'm waiting on a tow. Christian doesn't need to know I have Erika back safe with me and Drake and Ditch's corpses are long gone. Well, he doesn't need to know yet.

Inside the clubhouse, I search through the files in Christian's desk. I take the paperwork for Erika's old house. A few files back, I pull my file. There are properties that are solely in my name. These come with me. That's my income.

There's a red folder that catches my attention. Opening it, there's a list of properties on the Jackals side of town that Christian has or is working on taking ownership of. Erika's address was on the list. Flipping through the folder, I review the printouts of revenue from these properties. There's money he's been keeping for himself, keeping from the Serpents.

Seeing everything in front of me, I realize now why Christian's focus has been so strongly on winning the turf war against the Jackals. It's because he's winning the war and it's putting a hell of a lot of cash in his personal pocket. When you're this close, this hungry, do you betray your brother to cut your enemies off at the knees? That's what he's done.

GETTING HOME, I sit on the edge of the bed and watch Erika sleep. Her reddened cheeks now have bruises dappling her skin. I can't bring myself to think what would've happened to her if I hadn't put her first and come back for her. I would've made the biggest mistake of my life. I would've lost her and that thought creates a rage inside of me I'm unable to calm.

I'll do anything to protect her and I'll never hesitate to take another man's life who tries to hurt her. She's the only thing that matters to me. The one and only woman to bulldoze through my cement exterior and find the man worth loving inside. She's changed me and she doesn't know it. She's made me better. Made me see there are more opportunities than what's in front of us.

I'm going to make a great life for us together, but it can't be done here. The lifestyle I've lived is a road I can't continue on if I'm going to be the man she needs. It's time to move on and I know where that road is telling me to go. I only have one last thing to do before I climb on my Harley and never look back.

CHAPTER THIRTY

DOMINIC

"THAT'S THE LAST OF IT," Erika tells me, handing me a small bag full of our things. Camaro packed full, I close the trunk. Leaning against it, I bring her between my legs and hold her bruised face carefully as I kiss her.

"How you feeling?"

Beautiful golden hazel eyes look up at me, full of adoration and brimming with fear.

"I'm barely holding it together. I know you're going to confront him. I'm afraid you won't come back."

Gently brushing my thumb along her jaw, I steal a moment of pleasure, knowing how much she loves me.

"You don't need to be afraid. After this, we're free. We won't need to watch our backs. It's something I gotta do, for us."

"I love you so much." Head against my chest, she wraps her arms around my waist, holding me as tight as she can.

"You have no idea how much I love you. What I'll do for you."

Gaze to mine, she stares up at me, a new determination in her eyes.

"I know because it's the same as I'd do for you."

My lips take charge, kissing her with unrestrained passion, showing her how much I need her. Pulling back from her, her face is flushed. She's pushing against my cock, slipping her hands beneath my shirt.

"Do you want me inside you?"

I'm concerned she won't with what happened to her last night.

"Yes. I want to feel you inside me, loving me. I need it."

"So do I."

IN THE DARK, I wait, finger resting on the trigger of my gun. Minutes ago, his Harley rumbled into his driveway. Now the creaking of the hinges on his front door indicates his arrival. Not that I needed it. My eyes have adjusted to the lightless room.

With a flick of his hand, the living room light comes on after he's closed the door. He's not expecting me and his body jolts in surprise.

"Dom, what are you doing here?"

His eyes dart to my loaded gun.

"What's going on?"

"Cut the bullshit. Erika's alive. Drake and Ditch are dead."

Christian's a smart man. His expression remains the same.

"Tell me what happened."

"I don't need to waste our time explaining your well thought out plan. Only problem was you didn't expect me to choose her over the Serpents. I went back for her, planned on taking her with us. I knew something wasn't right when she didn't answer her phone. I rode straight to her old house where Drake and Ditch were beating her, getting her primed for them to rape her, then kill her. You were right. I would've gone after the Jackals. I would've taken out every one of them and not cared about going to prison. It would've got you just what you wanted—your enemies taken out, their turf for the taking, and your only remaining threat would be in jail."

"Threat," he scoffs.

"If I wanted to be President, all it would take is a few votes, and you'd lose everything. Greedy men get careless, Christian, and you've become one greedy son of a bitch."

Hand on his pistol, he's ready to pull it.

"Take your hand off it. I'm not going to shoot you."

Slowly, he withdraws his hand, confusion written on his face.

"What do you want?"

"To kill you with my bare hands. It's the only way I'll make peace with your betrayal."

When his hand reaches for his pistol, my eyes narrow.

"Reach for it again and I'll change my fucking mind." Standing, I aim the gun at his chest. "Slowly take it out and set it on the floor. It's your only chance of surviving. Your choice. Bullet or bare knuckles?"

Anger is etched across his brow, seething in his eyes, but it's nothing compared to the rage I'm barely containing. Leaning over, he drops the pistol. Eyes locked on his, I use my peripheral and kick it away. With his gun out of the way, I stick to my word and put mine back in my waistband.

Christian wastes no time attacking me. He lunges, arm swinging. Blocking his punch, I knock his arm back and slam the edge of my palm into his neck. It knocks him sideways, catching him off guard. Fist to his gut, I attempt to rob him of his breath. Coughing, he hunches over, only to rebound quick and charge forward. We both fly back and land on his coffee table, the weight of our bodies destroying the wooden table.

One punch lands on my face and I growl out my fury. Arm bent, hand to his chin, I force his face up, extending his neck. With one hard punch, I lay damage to his throat. He's struggling to breathe, scrambling to get off me. Grabbing across his chest to his shoulder, I buck my hip and roll us. Now over him, I unleash. Fist to face, I let it all out. Blood spatters from his broken nose, then mouth. Desperate coughs and rasps for breath fuel my rage. Another punch to his face and his eye is swollen shut. His disfigured face is difficult to recognize.

My arm lowers when I hear the struggle for air to be brought into his lungs. Bringing my face closer to his, I stare into his one open eye.

"You brought death to your own fucking door."

Withdrawing my switchblade from my jeans, I flick the knife open. Driving the metal into his stomach, I watch as it tears through his flesh and drains the life from his body.

Pulling my knife from his insides, I wipe the blood on his shirt. Blade away, I stand and retrieve my cell phone from my pocket. Mercy answers quickly.

"Christian's dead. The Serpents belong to you now. They need to know...if any of them come for us. I'll kill them...one by one."

EPILOGUE

DOMINIC

Riding my Harley up to the Kings clubhouse, I observe the silver skull and crown symbol just outside the door. Bike parked, I drop the kickstand and wait for Erika to step out of my Camaro. With a smile tugging at her lips, she takes my hand as we walk up the stairs, onto the porch. Through the front door, we enter a bar, and I take note of every man wearing leathers. A bald man with a spider web tattoo on his neck takes sight of me and measures me up.

"Who the hell are you?" he asks, suspicion laced in his tone.

A familiar frame turns my direction from the pool table they're at.

"Dominic fucking Xavier." Jake takes one look at me and smirks. "Easy, Axel. This man's family."

Setting his pool cue aside, he walks the few feet to where we stand.

"Your visit is a lot sooner than I expected. Everything all right?" He's reading me like a book. Something he always did when we were kids.

"That offer of an open door still good?"

Jake pats me on the shoulder, inviting us farther into the clubhouse. "Hell yeah it is. Let me get you both a beer."

TWO WEEKS LATER...

ERIKA CAN'T STOP GIGGLING as I hold my hands over her eyes, guiding her into our new home. Standing just beyond the front door, I remove my fingers. In front of me, her head turns left and right, then she swivels her body to face me.

"Is this ours?"

"Yeah, baby. It's our new home. I'm selling the house in Ohio."

"Dom..."

Her beautiful hazel eyes are bright with excitement and adoration.

"I'm gonna prospect for the Kings. We're never going back. We're starting a new life here."

She jumps into my arms and I cup her ass in my hands as her lips demonstrate what she's feeling in her heart. Putting her against the wall, I reach for her jean shorts. Her hands are already under my shirt, taking it off.

Letting her legs down, I move her shorts and underwear down off her hips. With a quick movement of her hands, she has my jeans undone and is sliding them off. The need between us is strong, uncontrollable. A craving we're eager to satisfy. Lifting her ass, her legs wrap around my waist. Coming together, I let out a groan of satisfaction. Each and every time I'm with her our love grows stronger. There's a primal ferocity she brings out of me. A need to claim. A need to possess.

This woman...my freedom.

Forever mine.

Forever my Sparrow.

THANK you for reading Clipped Wings! That story poured right out of me in exceptional speed and left me with a wicked writer's hangover. I will miss Dom, but thankfully he'll return in the Kings MC book 3! King of Kings, Nix's story is coming Jan 2020! To receive a live alert email when it releases, follow me on Bookbub or sign up for my newsletter at: bettyshreffler.com/subscribe

.   .   .

IF YOU LOVED CLIPPED WINGS, and want to check out my other sexy and suspenseful stories:

Enjoy a delightfully fun and sexy, fast paced office romance with combustible chemistry in My Hot Boss.

Or if you're looking for something passionate and heartbreakingly beautiful, fall in love with a swoonworthy cowboy in Fire on the Farm, or a charming and perfectly sculpted kickboxing instructor in Unbreak This Heart.

YOU CAN ALSO JOIN my Facebook readers' group, Betty's Book Beauties and Bad Boys, to connect with me personally, enjoy the fun, exclusive giveaways, and sneak peeks of future books! I'm in there once a week hanging out with my readers. :)

KEEP TURNING the pages if you want to check out my other sexy and suspenseful stories, where to stay connected with me, and what signings I'll be at next.

IF YOU ENJOYED CLIPPED WINGS, will you consider leaving a review? It's reviews from fans like you that help spread the word about my books, giving me the opportunity to keep writing them.

To book nerds everywhere;
you are my tribe
you make my dream possible
and for that
I thank you.

ALSO BY BETTY SHREFFLER

Kings MC Series

KING OF KINGS (Coming Jan 2020!)

Standalone Contemporary Romances

UNBREAK THIS HEART

MY HOT BOSS

FIRE ON THE FARM

Crowned and Claimed Series

CLAIMED ROYALTY

TWICE CLAIMED

FOREVER CLAIMED

Paranormal & Fantasy Romances

WHEN HUNTER MEETS SEEKER

Covenant Series

EMBRACE THE DAWNING

CRUEL TEMPTATION

DARK & BEAUTIFUL NIGHTS

bettyshreffler.com

ABOUT THE AUTHOR

Betty Shreffler is a USA Today and International bestselling author of romance. She writes sexy and suspenseful stories with hot alphas and kickass heroines with twists you don't expect. She also writes beautiful and sexy romances with tough women and their journeys at finding love. Betty is a mix of country, nerdy, sassy, sweet and a whole lot of sense of humor. She's a fan of photography, reading, watching movies, hiking, traveling, drinking wine, and all things romantic. She lives with her amazing hubs and fur babies; one rescue pup and a cat. If she's not writing or doing book events, then you can find her behind the lens of a camera, hiking in the woods, or sipping wine behind a deliciously steamy book.

Sign up for Betty's newsletter
@ bettyshreffler.com/subscribe

Join Betty's Facebook readers' group:
Betty's Book Beauties and Bad Boys

Visit Betty's website for signed paperbacks,

or see where she'll be for her next signing:
bettyshreffler.com

facebook.com/authorbettyshreffler

twitter.com/betty_shreffler

instagram.com/betty_shreffler

amazon.com/author/bettyshreffler

bookbub.com/profile/betty-shreffler